THE TORCH CAFÉ

A story of war, courage, and love, during the Blitz

By David M. Jacquez

This book is published by

Toltec Books

A publishing company owned

By David M Jacquez

Book Cover by Garret Moore

DEDICATION

THIS BOOK IS DEDICATED TO THE MEN AND WOMEN
OF ALL NATIONS, WHO SERVED AND FOUGHT
AGAINST FACISM IN WORLD WAR 2.

It is especially dedicated to the Towns Family of Texas,
and the Jacquez Family of New Mexico,
who answered the Battle Cry of Freedom.

For too many years, the sacrifices of the Mexican American
soldiers have rarely been discussed or portrayed on television or
in film. This book will make a small correction to that narrative.
Hopefully, in the future, as time and tides allow, other books will
make large corrections to that narrative.

CONTENTS

MESOAMERICAN WISDOM

TOLTEC BOOKS

AUTHOR'S PREFACE

I have always been fascinated by the history. When studying the broad strokes of history, an examination of war was required. After having studied the American Civil War, the next great conflict, that shaped the United States, was the second World War.

I spent several years gathering the oral histories and books that are available, concerning World War 2. As I read, and learned these stories, I realized that I would have to write this story as a play, and later, as a novel.

The day came when I told myself, it was time to do what all writers must do, and that was placing oneself in a chair, paper, and pen in hand, and commit ink to the page. My endeavors are now what you hold in your hand. I hope you enjoy.

THE PEOPLE

ERIC Thomas . . . . An English Major

BILL Morris . . . . US Army Colonel

ALICE Evans . . . . Sings at the Torch Café

Jenny MacDonald . . . . Singer at the Torch Café

Charles Ross . . . . Owner of the Torch Café

SCOTT MacDonald . . . . Jenny's Brother

Mark Anderson . . . . English General

Carlos Acat . . . . Boy Friend of Jenny

CHAPTER 1

ORDERS

Eric looked at the familiar door, with the old fashion, now slightly rusted knob. Eric used the knuckles of his right hand, to knock, receiving no answer, then knocked again, but harder. Hearing a voice, telling him to enter the office, Eric turned the knob.

"Reporting as ordered, Sir," Eric said, as he gave a snappy salute, his eyes meeting those of General Anderson, who was at the top of his chain of command.

Eric remained standing as he waited for General Anderson's Instructions.

General Anderson, looking down at Eric's file, then up, addressing Eric, "Major Thomas, Eric, first name. Eight years in the King's service. You have been recommended to me by the War office. As an officer, who will carry out his duties, with intelligence, energy, and foresight."

"Thank you, Sir." Eric paused, for a moment, " When at war, there is only one level of exertion, extreme." Eric responded.

"You are right." General Anderson said, as he closed Eric's file, placing his hands over the file. "What we are looking for, is an officer, with the ability to work with many different staff officers, from many different nations. The free French, Belgium's, Dutch and Poles, now stand beside England. Polish soldiers and pilot's have proven to be very effective fighters.

"Yes Sir. I understand."

"This England has survived because of our ability to rally the free peoples of Europe, against tyranny. Be it Napoleon, the Kaiser or this little corporal, this Hitler." General Anderson said, with slight anger, a low growl in his voice.

"Yes Sir."

General Anderson, continued, "I need a man who can talk to military officers of other nations. To rally them to our cause. You have toured Europe and spent time in the United States.?"

"Yes, Sir. Before I started my military career, before attending Sandhurst, I traveled in Europe, then North America. Visiting Canada, the United States, and Northern Mexico."

Gen. Anderson stopped for a moment looking down at the papers on his desk, then holds up a few pages in his hand.

"This is the war offices report, on the status of our arsenals."

"I have heard that our military resources are depleted."

"Depleted is a word for peace time. We face ruin. Our best weapons lay abandoned on the beaches of Dunkirk. Our men have returned with their lives. We have enough rifles to provide for half the regular army. The home guard drills with broom sticks." General Anderson starkly informed Eric, uncomfortable with the truth, as Eric stands stunned at the news.

"I understand, Sir."

"At this moment, we stand alone. Italy has declared war against England. Austria is now a possession of Germany. Poland has been bombed and overrun. The low land countries and France are occupied. These things you know."

General Anderson stands and walks for a few moments, coming up to Eric.

"It will be six months before any substantial arms can be delivered from our factories." General Anderson slowly said, with a tension to his voice; *knowing that there was only one man who could provide England with the arms and supplies needed.*

"Churchill has called on President Roosevelt to provide what assistance he can. Quietly and secretly, the President has sent a cargo ship of small arms. The home Guard is waiting at train stations, military bases, and town centers, for their weapons."

Eric started to feel pain in his leg, that Gen. Anderson noticed, when Eric grimaced.

"Please sit down Major."

"Thank you, Sir."

"The Prime Minister has addressed the President, in a most forceful and urgent manner. You must have heard his radio speech to the nation." General Anderson asked, as much as stating a truth. Knowing that an officer not listening to the PM's radio address would be a rarity. Seeing no reaction from Eric, he continued.

"Churchill felt he had a duty, and the right, to have it on the record, that if we are defeated, the Americans will face Germany and Europe, allied with other nations of the world, alone. With a population more numerous than America, and an industrial base equal or greater than the United States."

Eric, uncertain what to say, ' Sir, I know the perils."

General Marshall is now in discussions, with various military branches, as to extra equipment, that can be shipped to England. Again, being done without asking the Congress for funds and without any publicity. The same pacifist sentiment in England and Europe, that allowed Hitler to rebuild Germany's military, still holds sway in America."

"I spent some time in the United States, Sir. There is a large movement against any more involvement in European Wars. Many Americans blame the English for dragging them into the first world war." Eric said, with certainty in his voice.

"American opinion has started to change. With the bombing of Poland, the fall of France, and now the bombing of London." General Anderson starts to finger a cigar on his desk, still in its rapper. A present from the Prime Minister, that he looked at, almost to remember his instructions from Churchill. "Will American opinion mean more military support or action? No one knows." General Anderson softly said, twirling the cigar in his fingers for a moment.

"I would not wager, either way. Sir." Eric responded.

"That is one of the reasons, that I have chosen you. You understand

the Americans, better than most officers."

Eric stood tall, knowing he had been chosen for an important mission.

"An American, a Colonel William Morris, has been assigned to the American Embassy in London. To provide Washington with updates as to the events in Europe and the possibility of England being defeated by Germany. You are to be assigned to him, as our contact." General Anderson said, calmly looking at Eric.

"Yes sir." Eric said, still uncertain of any specifics.

"We believe this officer has access to the ears of the President. Convince him that we retain the fighting spirit. He must know that even in defeat, there is defiance." General Anderson almost shouting the last word.

What would you have me do, Sir. Eric asked. Still uncertain to his responsibilities.

"Be agreeable and differential to the Americans. As you have said, many are still in an isolationist mood."

" The Americans blame their Politicians for dragging them into the first great war. Telling them it was the war to end all wars. Many still suffer from mustard gas." Eric calmly said, remembering a group of War Veteran's at a 4th of July celebration.

"We must rally all, to our cause. Allies who believe as we do. If we fail, this Island, this England, may be bombed into ruin, or starved into submission." General Anderson said, getting angry at his own words, knowing their bitter truth.

"Sir, all that life and limb allow me to do, I shall do." Eric said.

"Major, there is one other thing you should know about Colonel Morris."

"Yes Sir. "

"Colonel Morris has delivered a letter. A request from Washington, for clarification. If England is invaded, and defeated, the Americans require assurances that his Majesties Navy will not be surrendered to Germany."

Eric stood in shock, as if a body blow had been thrown, with such a statement.

"We have given the most solemn pledge, that the fleet will sail to North America, with the war being waged from Canada. Major, I think that you now have a greater understanding of the peril of our current position. The battle that will soon fall upon us, will determine the survival of Christian Civilization."

"Yes Sir. I shall work closely with Colonel Morris." Eric said, with a gravity that had not been in his eyes before.

"You are dismissed, Major."

"Sir."

Eric turned and grabbed the door frame as he left, using it to balance himself, as he opened the door, and walked out, not wanting to show any signs of pain. Not wanting to be kept out of the war.

CHAPTER 2

ALICE AND JENNY

Eric and Bill walked into The Café. It has a mix of military and civilians attending the show. Men and women are drinking and talking, waiting for the show to begin.

Bill remarked, as he followed Eric, to their table, "It seems to be crowded. Must be a popular place."

"Standing room only in a little while. I thought that after a long day visiting air command, and military bases, a few drinks might be in order."

"You are right. I appreciate your briefing this morning. I also reviewed the file you provided. It gave me a clearer understanding of the current situation." Bill said as he continued to notice the makeup of the crowd.

"I have obtained permission to visit our monitoring stations on the coast. Some new technology that we have developed." Eric said as he stood at the table they were to occupy.

"Good." Bill answered, having already been told of radar, before leaving Washington.

It is starting to get noisy as Charles comes onto the stage.

"Welcome, welcome to The Torch Café. A night of entertainment, laughter, and a few kisses or tears, for those romantics amongst you."

A group of sailors stand up and cheer.

"I see a few sailors. We must have his Majesties navy at port.

Well, I know just the song. Let's bring on the beautiful and talented Jenny MacDonald, to entertain you. She's the land on the horizon, that you've been looking for.

A rousing cheer is given for Jenny as she comes on stage. Jenny has a British navy sailors' uniform on. Jenny blows kisses to the sailors and winks at a few of them.

As the music starts, so does Jenny, as she picks up the beat.

> ♪ Every sailor has one lass, in a port.
> A lady near a fort.
> And a wife, waiting for her sailor,
> to report. That he's back,
> and still, intact.
> Once, you sailed with canvas,
> catching every breeze.
> But went too far North,
> and started to freeze.
> Tahiti, Captain, if you please.
> It is Islands, I wish to see.

"Boys, join in the chorus."

> ♪ It's a sailor's life for me.
> To be, Sinbad of the seven seas.
> Sailing through the Pillars, of Hercules.

A sailor stands up, shouting, "Jenny, Marry me." Others also call out, joining in, "Marry me, Jenny."

Jenny laughing, "Marry a sailor? I prefer a tailor. Who stays on land!" Then pretending to fan herself. "But do bring back a

Chinese fan." The crowd roars their approval.

"Wow, she's a firecracker." Bill exclaimed.

"She's the same when you meet her." Eric said, as he watched Bill's face, showing delight.

"You know her?" Bill asked, as he continued to watch the show.

"*Yes.* I used to come here with a few of my mates. when it first opened. Before the war. I know several of the people who work here. Including Jenny, and Alice. The singers in the show."

As servers walk around taking drinks to the men and women, Jenny is surprised when she sees Eric. Jenny moves quickly down the steps of the stage, and over to the table.

"Eric, it's so good to see you. Alice told me what happened. France, the fighting. The Victoria Cross, and all. We're all so proud of you."

Eric gives a weak smile, not really wanting to talk about it. Bill looks at Eric with a bit of surprise. A greater level of respect.

"Glad to be back. Let me introduce you to Colonel Morris. I brought him out to see a little of the night life, in London."

"Nice to meet you, Colonel."

"My pleasure. Please have a seat."

Jenny sits down with Eric and Bill. Looking at the American Colonel for a moment, wondering what a Yank is doing in London.

"Colonel Morris." Jenny started to ask.

"How about just Bill?" He requested, as he smiled at Jenny.

"What brings a Yank to London at this time, Bill? Can't be a holiday.

Not in November. Not with the air raids going on."

"Well, I wanted to go to Brighten and lay on the beach with my umbrella. Enjoy the fine weather."

Jenny quickly looked at Eric, hearing a fake cough, coming from him.

"Don't think you'll get much out of this one." As he tapped the table, a sign Alice mention, about Eric when he was annoyed.

Jenny now knows not to ask, pulls her finger across her mouth, as if zipping her lips.

Charles, the owner of The Torch Café, sometime band leader and musician, comes onto the stage once again, to announce the next song.

Charles motions to the trumpet player to make noise, to get the attention of the crowd. The trumpet player blew his version of Gabriel's horn, "The Walls of Jericho". The crowd grows silent.

"Ladies and gentlemen, for the next performance, the lady that put the flame, in the Torch Café. The woman who put the fire, the burning desire, in every heart. Our own Alice Evans.

♪ My love, my lion, my soldier my sailor man.
In harm's way you stand.
Defending this land.
I cry at times, I don't know why.
I look at your picture, and give a sigh.
My love, my lion, my soldier man.
How do you hold a man,
when he is in a faraway land?
With each letter, I feel better. Taking my time,
lingering on each line. Each word, gentle and
soothing.
A lamb, I am, when in his arms.

♪   Your letter spoke of all our hopes. Our dreams,
      of so many things.
      A wedding day. Children at play.
      A garden to tend, a cottage to mend.
      My soldier man.
      My love, my lion,
      In harm's way you stand.
      Defending this land.
      Come back to me.
      Be brave, be careful,
      be my lover, again.

Alice then softly said, as if speaking to the wife's, or lover of those men who sat before her, making eye contact with some of the women. Needing their looks of reassurance. That they have also endured the loneliness, the uncertainty. Then turning to look at the men in uniform.

♪   "You are never alone. You are always in our
      thoughts and in our hearts."

"One day this war will end. Then our lives will begin again." Alice softly said.

The audience shouts their approval, the women in the crowd are seen with tears in their eyes, as they applaud.

Eric, Bill and Jenny are the first to stand and applaud. "Well, I know why they call this place the Torch Café," Bill said as he picked up his drink, tipping it towards Alice, as a silent toast to Alice, as she continued to stand on the stage. Turning to Eric, "That's the

Alice you know?"

Jenny waves to Alice. Alice sees Jenny and Eric at the same time, leaves the stage quickly and over, into the arms of Eric, giving him a long hug and kiss.

Bill realized that there is more than friendship between these two.

Alice then said, "I was so frightened when I heard what happened. I wrote letters, not knowing where you were. A Moments pause, a look of pain, and uncertainty. Alice spoke first, "I was so frightened when I heard what happened. I wrote letters, not knowing where you were. Pausing, a look of pain and uncertainty, covered her face. Tears following tears down her cheeks. "It was two months before I received a response."

"I was still in the hospital. Eric replied. "Then I spend time being debriefed. Sorry my love."

Eric started to gently touch Alice's arms, "I read all your letters. I thought I would surprise you."

Alice leans forward and gave Eric another hug. Eric then pulled back, wanting to introduce Bill.

"Alice, I want to introduce you to Colonel Morris. He's an American officer who is stationed here."

Alice smiled and said, "How do you do."

Bill smiled broadly, "After that performance, very well indeed."

Bill looked at Alice, with admiration. Noticing her green eyes, burnet hair, and fair complexion, and a smile that seemed to come easily, as she spoke.

"I've heard that song before, but never like that, Bill said. " You have a beautiful voice."

"Thank you," Alice answered. Alice turned her head, slightly standing up, trying to see where Charles was. "I need to talk to Charles. I'm sure he'll give me the rest of the night off. Jenny, can you stand in for a few extra songs?" Alice said, knowing that she and Jenny often covered for each other.

"You know I cannot say no." Jenny, turning to Eric, "Eric, so good to have you back. I do have to leave. I'm next." Jenny ran off to the stage.

"Well, I think that's my cue to bow out. You've got a lot of catching up to do. And three's a crowd." Bill said as he took another quick glance at Alice, as Eric waved goodbye to Charles.

Turning to Bill, "My driver will take you back." Eric said as he offered his hand to Bill, who quickly took hold, giving a firm handshake.

"I will see you tomorrow as planned. I'm glad you enjoyed the show. Eric said as his duties and responsibilities once again took hold of him."

"Great show. Wouldn't have missed it. Thanks for showing me around."

As Bill leaves the café, Alice comes over, now covered by her long coat.

Eric asked, "Shall we go somewhere?" Eric saw a slight tension in Alice's body, hearing it in her voice."

Alice puts her fingers to Eric's lips and stopped him from speaking. "No, just home. Some tea and a few moments with you. That is all I want, all I need."

Eric reached over to place his hand upon Alice's hand, feeling how warm it was. "We will wait and talk. When the car is back, I shall obey your command, and take you home."

Alice, hesitating , then asked, "You will not be sent back, not with your injury?"

Eric smiled and announced, "I have been assigned to Head Quarters, here in London. " A tension dropped from Alice's Shoulders."

Charles walked over to greet Eric, motioning to the bartender that his usual drink be brought to him.

Eric stood, offering his hand, as Charles approached the table.

"Eric, Welcome home." Charles said.

"Good to be home" Eric said.

"That was all I could think of, when I returned from the first war." Charles said, then hesitated, not wanting to open recent memories. Fresh wounds. " I know what you have seen. No man who has ever seen the face of war can forget. or would ever want to see it in his own homeland."

Eric grimly nodded.

Charles continued. "Thank you for your service. I, and all of England stand beside you, and those who serve."

"Alice, Eric, Jenny, when this war is over, after your wedding, I will close the Torch Café, for three months. We will all go our merry ways. I shall go back to New Orleans and play Jazz, then see if I can put a band together, performing on a paddlewheel Riverboat, up and down the Mississippi. A fond dream I have always had."

Alice asked, amused, and excited by the idea, "Will I be able to sing,' ' looking at Jenny and her interest, excitement. "With Jenny?"

Eric quickly said, "I shall buy the first ticket." The driver enters the Torch Café, and stands a moment, as Eric sees him.

Eric and Alice leave as Charles returns to the Stage. Charles waves to them and a few in the crowd applaud as Alice walks by.

CHAPTER 3

ALICE'S FLAT

Alice opened the door, as Eric follows her in. Eric grabbed Alice by her shoulders, turning and pulling her back towards him, then leaned over her shoulder, kissing her, then held her in his arms. Then again, giving Alice a strong, lingering hug and kiss.

"That is all I've been longing for, dreamed of. Just to hold you, kiss you." Eric said.

"My dearest love," Alice replied as she placed her hands on his face, "We dream the same dream."

Eric kisses Alice again, who returned the kiss. Then pulls back a little. "Let me prepare some tea, as I have promised you."

Alice walks to the kitchen area and starts to make some tea.

Eric, just sitting, watching Alice, as she moved around the Kitchen. "Such a simple thing. Just to sit quietly and have some tea. How I've missed it."

"I talked to your mum last week." Alice said as she placed the teacups on the table, with some warmed-up pie. "She told me how lucky you are to be alive."

"It seemed a frightful injury at the time, but the doctors were very good. Although I must say, my days of doing the Jitterbug, may be over."

An air raid siren is heard, as Alice, in an involuntary motion, looks up.

"It seems we've in for another blackout." Alice said, as Eric moved towards Alice, and tells her to be ready to move to the hallway, where there is more structural support, from walls, if bombs are heard falling, hitting.

The air raid warden is heard bellowing, shouting to various houses along the street. "Put that light out." The air warden shouted. "Don't make me climb those stairs."

The air warden continued to walk, shouting out now and then. "Put that light out, before you're fined."

Alice moves over and closes the curtain a bit tighter, as Eric walked over to help her. Alice grabs a flashlight and looks at Eric. The lights go out.

"Most people go to the shelters; others stay in their flats. Some of us go to the roof tops to watch."

"That's not safe."

"What is safe? Where is it safe? I will not hide from this war." Alice said, with a defiance in her voice that Eric had not heard before.

Alice pauses for a few moments, her lips trembling as she looks at Eric.

"Joan was so frightened by the air raids. She went into a back-yard shelter each time. A firebomb hit , a building fell, blocking the exit from the shelter. When they finally dug them out, no one was alive.

I cannot go into the shelters."

"I hadn't heard." Eric quietly said as he got up from his chair, knowing that Alice and Joan had been childhood friends. Eric got behind Alice, giving her a protective hug. Alice placed her hands on top of Eric's hands.

Alice stood, then motioned to Eric, to follow her as she grabbed a flashlight from a small table near the door. Alice waited till Eric is in the hallway, and closes the door, leaves her flat unlocked, and goes up the stairs.

CHAPTER 4

ROOF ABOVE ALICE'S FLAT

Eric sees some flashlights pointing to the stairs in front of him. They both hear people on the stairs and coming from other voices on the roof. The others cannot be seen, only their footsteps and voices heard.

The Landlady came out of her ground floor flat, and from the bottom of the stairs, shouted at those going up to the roof, "You're supposed to go to the shelters, not the roof. Well, just make sure to turn the flashlights off."

Alice turns to Eric, "Do not answer her. The Landlady is a busy body and will tell the blackout Warden who we are."

"Understood. She will not come up.

"No. As soon as the sirens sound, she heads to the basement."

Alice and Eric are on the roof.

"Once, the fires were so bright, they lit up the sky. You would see the planes falling, the houses burning. Knowing that men, women, and children were dying."

Alice grows silent for a moment, as if seeing into that terrible night.

"They only attack at night now. September was the heaviest bombing. All of London seemed to be on fire. The Dome of Saint Paul's, could be seen in the glow."

"From my hospital bed, I could hear the sound of the bombs as they fell, the explosions." Eric said, as he grabbed hold of Alice's hand.

"We must live, Eric. I must believe that sanity can return to this world. That the daily horror of this war will end."

The anti-aircraft artillery and search lights move, covering the sky. As formations of bombers are found, the search lights merge, as the air batteries intensify. All remain silent, as the bombers pass over.

"I visited an air base this morning, with that American Colonel you met. I hope he is watching the fireworks. That we continue to defend this island."

Many start to head back to their flats, as Eric and Alice wait till most of them have gone down. "You seem to be escorting him around." Alice said, as much a question, as a statement. "He must be an important man."

"More so than you might imagine. He will be reporting to Washington. His opinion, his report, is of critical importance. There is no more I can say about Colonel Morris."

Eric and Alice move closer together, their shadows merging. The sirens give an all-clear sound. Motioning to Eric, with a touch of her hand, "We can go down now."

Alice turns on her flashlight, as she grabs hold of the handrail, taking the first step, down the stair well, and goes down with Eric following. Gently touching the hand of Eric, Alice leads him back to her flat.

"You'll get me in trouble going on the roof. If the authorities find out, I'll be fined and so will you."

The Landlady calls out, trying to determine who went up on the roof.

Mrs. Johnson, was that you on the roof top? Would you please answer me?

All remains quiet as the tenants go back into their flats.

"There are no secrets in this building. If you talk to her, whatever was said, will be in your neighbors ears the next day."

"Rents due tomorrow. Don't forget." The Landlady said.

Eric, getting mad, not willing to sneak or hide from her, steps out of the shadows with his military uniform on. The Landlady recognizes Eric as the man she saw in the newspapers, who won the Victoria Cross. "Meant no offence Sir, but It's the law."

"Yes, I agree." Eric said. "Yet, there are times it is much safer on the roof, than on a burning street. I have fought in the ruined cities of France, as they burned. A roof top view provided me with information as to the best direction to attack or evacuate the building and regroup."

"I understand Sir. My apologies."

Eric turned to Alice who has a slight smile on her face. "There is more truth to that statement, than she might imagine."

CHAPTER 5

THE RAG

Eric and Alice entered the Officer's club, the Rag. Alice is on the arm of Eric. It is to be a night of dinner and soft music. They are taken to a table.

"It's a night I have promised you. A year is a long time to have a woman wait, for such an evening."

Alice gives a loving smile at Eric and holds his hand for a moment and squeezes it. "I would have waited forever."

Eric smiles then realizes what pain Alice would feel if something should happen to him. "Alice, if something should happen to..."

Alice quickly puts her fingers to Eric's lips.

Alice firmly said, "We will not talk of such things. This is the night you promised me."

"You are right." Eric gave Alice a look of deep love, that kind of look he gave to Alice, before the war started, when he proposed marriage, vowing to give to Alice, his all, body, heart and soul.

"Alice, I have asked that American Colonel you met, to join us for dinner. I wanted to introduce him to some of my mates, the other officers."

Eric pauses for a moment and once again grabs hold of Alice's hand, as she assured him with a look, that she accepted his wishes.

"I understand." Alice said, as her hand covered his.

The band starts playing. Three couples get up to dance. Bill enters the room, and walks over to Eric and Alice. "Sorry for being a few minutes late."

"Not at all. We have just ourselves arrived. Please have a seat." Alice said, trying to be friendly to this American.

Bill sits down and looks at Eric and feels like a third wheel again.

Eric addressing Bill, "I wanted to introduce you to some of the other officers, in a more informal setting. In a little while this place will start to fill, and I expect that I will see a few of my mates. They wanted to welcome me back.

"Well, if it were me, I would settle for kisses from my girl, and tell my "Mates" I would see them later."

"I have already shared a good night kiss. Eric has been rewarded as women are known to do." Alice said, sweetly smiling, knowing all the implications of her words.

"Eric is a lucky man."

More officers, some with their ladies, come into the Rag.

"Colonel, there are some of the officers that I have served with. Let me introduce you." Eric motioned to Bill, to follow him, as he spoke to Alice. "If you would excuse us."

Alice smiles and nods her head. Eric and Bill got up from the table, and went over to the bar, where Eric's mates are standing. Bill, with a slight laugh, as he dodged a chair being pulled out, navigating himself to the bar, telling Eric, "You would not catch me leaving a table with such a pretty woman, just sitting alone. I hope you do not have the kind of wolves we have in the states."

Two officers notice Eric and the American uniform of Bill as they walk towards the bar. As Eric approached, he brightened up, seeing the two officers he had served with. Eric noticed that Martin had been promoted to Captain.

"Hello Jim, Martin, I am glad you could come."

Jim responded, "Wouldn't have missed it."

Martin also extended his hand, offering his own greetings, "Good to see you! And back on your feet. Did not think the Jerry's could keep you down."

"Jim, Martin, allow me to introduce you to Colonel Morris. He's been assigned to the American embassy, as part of their military staff.

"Good to meet you, Colonel."

"Likewise." Bill answered.

Martin, putting down his drink, taking a step forward, also extended his hand. "My pleasure, Sir."

"Mine too." Bill simply said.

"How's that leg healing?" Jim asked. "Must have been a nasty wound, to keep you in the hospital for so long."

"It's Healing. The doctors have told me to be patient."

Martin then asked, "Still postponing the marriage?"

"We both feel it is the right decision. At least till this war is over. With everything rationed, it is impossible to stage a decent wedding, and reception."

Bill, spoke up, not forgetting his assignment, and why he was in London. "Eric has told me that he served with Martin, in France."

"I had that honor." Martin said. "Eric twice led the attack against the Jerries, regaining a crossroad. Till we were ordered to fall back, as a rear guard."

"I have been briefed by your military on the events in France. Eric has informed me of what he witnessed on the battlefield."

"Colonel Morris is here to gather information for the Chief of staff, in Washington." Eric announced.

"I now have a good understanding of what happened, and the current situation." Bill answered, as he finished his drink, nodding his head to the bartender, for a refill.

"It's a lot of information to digest." Jim said, as he finished his fourth drink.

"The Major has been very helpful in allowing me to tour your military air bases and gather information."

"Do you think the United States will enter the war?" Jim asked.

Bill responded, with some uncertainty in his voice. "I think it may happen in the future. But as most sane people believe, war is to be avoided."

Jim remarked with some disdain in his voice, "In the future? There might not be a future. If America waits." Jim paused, starting to notice Eric looking at him.

Eric, in a flash of fury, "Jim, I do not appreciate your attitude. With or without the American's, this nation must fight on. There is no alternative."

"Sorry Eric. It is common knowledge, the speeches of the Prime Minister. His calls for assistance, that the New World. Must save the Old World. Jim said, realizing he had crossed an unknown line.

"Eric is right." Bill agreed. " There is no alternative. Herr Hitler is a mad man. He's word, is worthless." Bill remarked, having emphasized the word, "worthless", as he announced his opinion of the little corporal in Berlin.

"And what have you learned, Colonel?" Martin now asked, wanting to turn down the heat.

"A few weeks after becoming the Chancellor of Germany, he imprisoned or killed off, all his political rivals. The Germans call it the 'Night of the Long Knives.' We play hardball politics, but not that hard."

"And that was only the beginning." Martin said, as he now started to pay more attention to the American Colonel.

"That's for sure." Bill remarked, with a low whistle, hardly audible, that was followed by a short laugh. "The little corporal assassinated the leader of Austria, arranged for agent provocateurs in Czechoslovakia and Norway, then marched right in, as if he owned the place."

"And now he does." Martin said, shaking his head in both sadness and annoyed disappointment, that both countries had fallen so quickly.

"And you would suggest?" Jim asked, not really expecting any helpful suggestions.

Bill forcefully answered, as his face hardened, "Hold on - fight on. There are no other options. The Nazi's now occupy the Channel Islands. Before the hordes of Hitler's Huns, enter London, Kill them. Before the sounds of Jack Boots are heard marching down cobbled streets, kill them." Bill stopped a moment. Waiting to see how Martin and Jim would respond. Eric nodded his head.

"The terrible bombings of Poland, the swift defeat of the low countries, and France. Now, the constant bombing of London, is changing America's attitude." Bill firmly stated, more than giving his opinion, but indirectly offering support, that he knew Roosevelt shared.

"I hope you are right." Martin said, as he took another drink.

"For years the America First party held large rallies, with Charles Lindbergh barnstorming across the nation, giving speeches, against any more involvement, in European wars. Many have listened."

Martin quickly said, "Your Lindbergh has visited Herr Hitler."

"Yes, I know. So did Mosley, the leader of the Black Shirts. I think Hitler was at his wedding."

Jim stiffened, not thinking any Americans knew about Mosley. Bill then continued, glancing at his table now and .

"I also know that seventy percent of the American people now believe that we will eventually be in this war. The transfer of military hardware continues to Britain. Planes and Battle ships are being talked about in America's Newspapers. Letters to the Editor seem to be in support of America joining the war. Although most of the Letters seem to be from Canadians who are working in the United States." Bill said with a smile, knowing of the relationship between England and Canada.

Bill, wanting to return to the table, to be with Eric and Alice, but seeing the interest his words and views had on Jim and Martin, continued the discussion, "There could not have been committee hearings, on the transfer of such weapons, just six months ago."

Martin then mentioned, "We have paid a price for those weapons, with gold, and stock in American companies. Our people have surrendered their wealth to his majesty's government, to buy weapons. Military bases have been transferred, should I say leased to the United States. "

"That is true. Yet, how useful is Bermuda, Jamaica, and the Bahama's to England, in its fight against Germany?" Bill remarked.

"So, you think we made a good bargain? Jim asked Bill, not expecting any answer.

"Yes. The transfer of such military equipment is the act of a belligerent nation, not a neutral nation as we profess to be. Churchill and Roosevelt have drawn the United States and England closer, but slowly."

Eric nods his head and Martin remained silent. Eric notices that Alice is looking at him and knows he is needed at the table as some drinks start to arrive.

"Gentleman, I cannot leave Alice alone for too long. Please excuse me."

Bill, Jim and Martin nod their heads as Eric walks towards Alice.

"You seem to have a good grasp of this war." Jim said, knowing that more Americans who thought as the Colonel did, could only help England. Yet Jim felt this American Colonel, having just arrived, was taking on airs, speaking on issues he could not be privy to.

"I would like to think so as that is why I'm here." Bill said to the surprise of both Jim and Martin.

Jim, with a slight bit of disdain in his voice. "Any good advice you might give us?"

"No, not really. You have a fine military and I believe that they have prepared for those events that are most dangerous."

"Such as?" Jim said, with a tint of superiority in his voice.

Bill looks at Jim, wondering if he is being rude or just ignorant.

"If Spain moves away from its neutrality, and sides with Germany, Gibraltar will be lost. Bill paused, picking up his drink. "With North Africa in the hands of Vichy France, who continues to shell Gibraltar, after you attacked the French fleet at Oron, you may be closed off from the Mediterranean, just as the Italians move towards the Suez Canal."

"Any more good advice?" Jim asked, in a jesting voice, before Martin could shut him up, realizing the American Colonel was getting angry.

"The Canary Islands are a dagger pointed at the heart of England! Do not allow them to become a base for U-boats. You will be starved to death." Bill smiled for a moment, seeing the surprise on Jim and Martins face. "But of course, your admiralty has already prepared for that possibility, as they have now informed me."

Martin and Jim look stunned at Bill's grasp of the situation and start to realize that he is not just a military officer attached to the embassy. Why would the admiralty have to explain anything to this American?

Eric is waving to Bill, to come and join them.

"Gentleman, please excuse me, Drinks are being served, and I miss your fine Scotch." Bill moved away from the bar and returned to join Eric and Alice, who was the first to speak to Bill.

"I hope they did not bore you.?" Alice said.

"Not at all. We had an interesting discussion on the political and military events that have created the current situation."

"And you believe?" Alice asked.

"That Herr Hitler makes the Mad Hatter in Wonderland, look like the most rational of men."

Eric and Alice laugh as do some on the surrounding tables who have listened in on the conversation, having noticed the American uniform.

"I will toast to that," Eric said, still slightly laughing at Bill's comment. "Cheers everyone."

Alice, Eric and Bill raise their glasses.

As the band starts to set up, a band member, noticing Alice, talks to the Band Leader, pointing to Alice. The band leader, Lance, walked over to Alice.

"Alice, so good to see you." Lance said, "A little bit like old times." Lance continued loudly. A habit he had developed, from yelling at a father who was mostly deaf.

" Hello Eric." Lance said.

Alice then turned to Bill, "Colonel Morris, this is Lance Logan, the band leader. I toured with the band, before the petrol rationing stopped all that."

Standing, with his outstretched hand, "Good to meet you, Lance." Bill and Lance shook hands, as Lance then turned to Alice for a moment, then asked a question.

"Alice, our singer, has not yet arrived. The band was wondering if you might help us with a song or two?"

Alice having noticed that no singer was on stage, and her intuition having already told her what Lance would ask, Alice immediately announced, "I would love to."

Eric, with a slight protest, "It's your night off."

With a stern look, "Eric, I cannot say no, not to these men!"

Alice walked towards the stage with some in the audience clapping, as they recognized her. As Alice greeted a few of the band members, Lance grabbed the microphone; he started to address the audience.

"Ladies and Gentlemen, we have a surprise for you. Many of you know Alice Evans, from the days she toured with the band. She has given in to our requests, that she perform a song tonight. Please welcome her to the stage."

Alice smiled as she took center stage, then addressed the band, "Play, 'After the Storm is Over.' "

Lance and Alice sharing the song and the microphone. Lance first grabbed the microphone, then started the song, talking more than singing the first few verses.

♪   A little girl asked, not long ago. "When will the planes stop? When will my daddy come home?"

Alice started to sing quietly.

♪   "After the storm is over, after the lightning is gone. After the clouds of darkness, give way to the break of dawn."

Lance then approached the microphone, continuing the song.

♪   "Many a child's laughter will give way to dance and song. After the storm is over, after the lightning is gone.

Alice and Lance once again join their voices.

♪   After the clouds of darkness, give way to the break of dawn.
"After the storm is over, after the planes are gone. After the clouds of darkness, give way to the break of dawn.
Many a lover's embrace will bring a wedding. A child to

Alice stops singing, surprising the band who stop playing. Alice firmly, yet in a soft voice, "This England is my home. I know no other. Shoulder to shoulder, bolder and bolder, we march to flutes, bagpipes, and drums, as one."

Lance, once again talking more than singing.

"Piccadilly's bright lights. Pubs, to gather as mates. Kites and Bicycle's in the park."

Lance then shouted out, "Come on, Everyone, you've heard it on the wireless." Alice, leading the crowd, started them singing.

♪ "After the storm is over, after the lightning is gone. After the clouds of darkness, give way to the break of dawn. Many a child's laughter will give way to dance and song. Many a lover's embrace, till the break of dawn.

Wild cheers went up as Lance and Alice bow, then Alice goes back to her seat as the audience continues to stand and applaud. Bill is still applauding until Eric pulls back the chair for Alice to sit.

As she sat, Eric exclaimed, "That was wonderful.

Bill immediately followed up with, "Just beautiful."

Alice answered with a smile that said "Thank You, and "I like You"; with a look. Looks that women have, with their thousand faces, faces women bring out, when needed to obtain their desires, their wishes from men.

The music started up again. It is a slow love song, with soft music playing as a few couples got up to dance.

Alice studied Eric's face, to see if there was any recognition of the song. Alice then asked, "That was our first dance, do you remember?"

"Yes, Love." Eric answered, "It was the first time I held you in my arms. I remember. Eric got up, and walked behind Alice, as Bill lifted his glass as they started to dance.

"It's been so long." Alice murmured.

" Just to hold you. To dance with you is all that I desire." Eric responded, as he grasped her hand, interweaving their fingers together.

Eric and Alice continue to dance, then on a turning movement, Eric grimaces and grabs hold of his leg. Bill sees what has happened, moves quickly. "I hope you don't mind if I cut in." Bill asked.

Eric, recovering, then said, "Please. Alice loves to dance, and I would have her enjoy her first night out."

Alice asked, "Eric, are you all right?"

"I'm fine, just not ready for those turns. I will sit for a moment. Please finish the dance with Bill." Eric then slowly walked back to the table.

Bill and Alice started to dance as Alice looked over at Eric, as he returned to the table and sat down, then smiling at Alice. The music stopped and Alice moved swiftly back to the table.

Alice leaned towards Eric, "Let's go home. I have had enough dancing for the night."

"I'll be fine. Just need to rest for a moment. Let's at least enjoy the music."

Alice looked concerned and continued to sit beside Eric. Just then, an officer walked over to the table and addressed Eric. "Hello Major. Sorry to disturb you, but the PM has requested your presence."

"My God, its 11:00 pm." Eric said, a bit stunned by the request.

"He often works until three and four in the morning."

Eric turned to Alice, not really knowing what to tell her.

Alice answered for him. "You report to Churchill? Eric, you must go immediately."

Bill chimed in. " I would not keep him waiting. Might be a shot of Scotch, in it, for you."

The Driver, knowing that some Americans disapproved of liquor, having outlawed it, not many years before, considered Churchill, as they once considered US Grant, a drunk.

"Thank you, Alice. We'll plan for another night. Bill, would you escort Alice back to her place."

"Yes, of course." Bill quickly answered.

"Alice loves to dance, make sure she enjoys the evening." Eric asked of Bill, as Eric immediately turned to Alice, with disappointment in his voice, his eyes giving a look of sorrow.

Eric takes hold of Alice's hand and kisses it. Then follows the British officer.

"He's a fine man, Alice. You're a handsome couple together."

"Thank you. Colonel Morris, I do wish to go home. Would you mind?"

"Not at all. Although I did promise Eric, I would keep you on the dance floor."

"Then one more dance, so that you may keep your promise."

Bill helped Alice with her chair, and they started to dance. A slow dance, as Alice smiles for a moment and starts to feel the music.

Siren's sound as an air raid is announced. People start to leave for the shelters. Lance grabbed the microphone. to announce, "Come on, everyone. To the shelters. We will play for you there. The Jerry's are not going to stop the music."

All started to move to the shelter, as Alice just sat there. Bill got up and waited for her.

Bill stood there , looking at Alice. "Alice?" Bill simply said, as both a question and a prompt.

"I cannot go into the shelters. I will wait here." Alice exclaimed in a manner that told Bill not to question her decision. Bill sat down again. "Then I shall wait with you."

The sound of the bombing, and concussions, blew out two windows, as the lights started to flicker. The sound of the bombs grew closer, as a near hit made Alice jump, as Bill also leaped up from his chair. Alice hugged Bill for a few moments. The lights turned on as Alice pulled away from Bill. "Sorry Colonel." Alice said.

"These raids unsettle most people. I served in the first war, and saw the bravest of men, with fear on their faces, during an artillery barrage. Then get up and move forward.

"Thank you, Colonel, Alice softly said.

Please, call me Bill.

"Bill, I believe the music' and dancing, is over for the night. If I might ..."

"Yes, of course."

CHAPTER 6

THE BUNKER

Eric walked down the corridor, with its Reddish orange glow that came from the light bulbs that had been placed every ten feet, giving just enough light to allow the names next to the door to be read. Eric, seeing a cabinet minister leaving an office, then passing a door marked War Room, he proceeded forward. Seeing a door marked Churchill, Eric entered as a secretary in a military uniform greeted him, as he entered.

"Sir, may I assist you?" She asked, hardly looking up, delivering the same line, in the same monotone voice as she often did, when hearing the door open.

Eric, looking around, never having been in the Bunker, then quickly answered, "I was brought here. Told to report to the Prime Minister.

The secretary getting up, said, "Please have a seat, I shall tell the PM that you are here.

He is finishing up his discussions with BB.

Eric nodded his head, and took a seat, as a middle-aged man left the room, with the secretary quickly saying, "See you tomorrow, Brenden."

Brenden, looking back, over his shoulder, asking her, "Did you like the stories on the wireless ? I hope you are still enjoying the news stories?"

"Oh yes," she quickly answered.

Brenden turned to her as he closed the door, "Good."

The Secretary motioned to Eric that he should enter Churchill's office.

As Eric entered the under-ground office of the PM, he saluted Churchill, who then addressed Eric immediately, seeing his dress uniform, "Hopefully you enjoyed part of the night."

"Yes Sir." Eric responded.

"I have heard that you have confronted men who seem to have made a halfhearted effort in their duties."

"I have continued to talk to all the officers that I meet; impressing upon them the need to instill a will to fight in their men. The necessity to confront all defeatism.

"Victory must be perceived in the mind and in the heart, before it can be won on the battlefield." Churchill gruffly said with a conviction that would allow no misinterpretation.

"Yes, Sir."

Eric pauses, for a moment wanting to tell Churchill, in his own way, that he understands that victory must be achieved.

"Sir, I have seen my first bombing of London, from a roof top. I have redoubled my efforts."

"I once watched from a roof top myself. Until my staff grew to excited in their requests that I leave for a safer place."

"Yes, Sir."

"And Colonel Morris? For that is why I have requested this meeting. Reports do not give the measure of the man."

"I have collaborated closely with Colonel Morris. Providing him with the information that he has requested. He asks the most astute questions. He is well informed on the current situation. As you suggested, he seems to support us. He believes it's only a matter of time, before the Americans find themselves in this war.

"I am of the same opinion." Churchill said, as he pushed aside some papers, looking for his intelligence briefing. "The president has called for a military draft, and improvements to America's armaments. Many who were isolationists now grow silent."

Eric now told of his discussions with other Americans. "The American Radio announcers, covering the blitz, add a darker tone to their coverage. Many support us. Yet, few wish to offer their sons and daughters, in a faraway war."

"What catalyst or event that must happen, to bring the Americans into this war, I know not. I do not think the President knows. We must allow events to unfold. Till then, we fight on."

"Yes, Sir."

"Roosevelt is now in the process of attempting to pass a bill for fifty Destroyers. War ships, to be transferred to His Majesties Navy. They are sorely needed. The German's have now put into commission a great battleship, they call it the Bismarck. We must keep it bottled up in the North Sea or destroy it."

"Yes, Sir."

"Continue as you have. Treat him as a fellow officer, as if he has served with you. He may in the days to come. We have many things in common with the Americans. Let him perceive that as you spend time with him."

"Yes Sir."

Churchill is a little moody, knowing that this great and terrible war could have been stopped.

"It should have never happened." Churchill quietly said. Eric, not sure if Churchill was addressing him, immediately asked.

"Excuse me, Sir?"

"This damnable war. It should have never happened. Yet the horrors of the first war, held to strong a hold on people's minds. Three quarters of a million men of England - killed. So many more injured. The French with more than a million dead.

"Yes, Sir. No one wanted to believe it could happen again. It was to have been the war to end all wars. Now, just twenty years later." Eric's voice trails off, "One man has been allowed to start this terrible war. The little corporal could have been stopped when the Germans marched into the Ruhr. Yet, the French, the Allied contingents had already been evacuated."

"The dye had been cast. The allies who had defeated Germany, remained undecided, as to their actions. With Germany, largely undamaged after the first war, they remained a united people. The largest "tribe" in all of Europe. Major, there will not be, "Peace in our time." Churchill, hearing the door to his office opened, he slightly shook his head, his way of informing his secretary that he was not to be disturbed. Churchill continued his discussion with Eric, who was surprised that he was having such a talk with the Prime Minister.

"The refusal of the United States Senate to support the Treaty of Guarantee, that President Wilson had signed, would have insured the defense of France, and the support of a demilitarized zone.

"We allowed the Hun to rearm and did nothing. They are once again at our throats. I would have them on their knees."

Eric shouted out, "Sir, yes Sir."

"It is a terrible truth that we must acknowledge. In a strange kind of logic, this nation and Europe told themselves, if we disarmed, the Germans would have no need to build more arsenals.

Churchill just shook his head, "The weakness of the peaceful and virtuous, allowed the malice of the wicked to gather more strength, and more weapons.

Churchill starts to get mad, stern in his gaze. Churchill quickly stood, then, as if he was at a speaking podium, or addressing the House of Commons, spoke forcefully, allowing Eric to hear and forever remember the roar.

"We inflicted a thousand cuts upon ourselves. He paused and walked for a moment.

"The Oxford Union debates. Damn them. That Englishmen should debate if they should fight for king and country. That such a motion should be made. I wanted to send a white feather to each person who voted in favor of such a motion.

"It was a disgrace Sir. I could not believe that the Oxford Pledge was passed."

"My son tried to have the offending words removed but was greeted with jeers and hisses. The men of Oxford will now have to wash away that infamous vote, with their blood."

Churchill seemed tired for a moment. Then in a quieter voice, "We became our own executioners." Churchill shook his head again, still not believing in the folly of men.

Churchill relaxes for a moment and sat down. Looking at Eric.

"It was more than Oxford, Sir. It was the sentiment of the country, for a time.

"Yes, it is true. It was a desire for peace. The people allowed the uninformed and disillusioned, to follow a path that would have taken this England to total disarmament.

Eric, still surprised that Churchill was having such a discussion with him, continued, knowing that this was a privileged moment.

"They could have been stopped! Now, rather than working to recover from a terrible depression, I must order millions of gas masks to be made. Having to spend untold sums to defend this island, this England."

Churchill stopped abruptly, not wanting to burden Eric, with all his concerns, and knowing he needed to prepare for more meetings, ended his discussion with Eric.

"Thank you for your report. You are dismissed Major."

Yes, Sir.

Eric salutes and starts to leave, as Churchill addressed him once again, bringing Eric to a halt. "Major, *I know you may feel uncomfortable, being a "guide" for an American officer, and news broadcasters, yet I can* assure you that you have been assigned one of the most critically important tasks that must be accomplished successfully.

Eric slightly nods his head. "Yes Sir."

"Take Colonel Morris to the war situation room. He should see that we are prepared for any event. Then take a day off with the Colonel. Take him back to that Café he so much enjoyed. Let him see that life continues."

"Yes, Sir."

Churchill, started to get angry, "We must fight on. The Germans want to push London into confusion, chaos, and paralysis. They want to bend us to their will."

Eric, recalling the fighting in France, the lives, the friends lost.

The broken leg, almost lost, matched Churchill's anger, shouting out, "Never."

Churchill paused for a moment, wondering if he should tell the Major his most recent fears. That the Germans were bringing hundreds of barges for the invasion of England. Then deciding that the urgency of the moment, demanded that the major be informed.

"The Germans are moving barges, and anything else that floats, down the coast of France, finding safe harbor opposite our shores. We may well be fighting the battle of the English Channel, soon. All must share in the sacrifices, on the altar of freedom. I have seen age old privileges, rank and wealth laid down.

Eric nods his head, with a look of calm.

"Sir, if I might ask?"

"Why a request to meet with you?"

"Yes, sir. Most of my reports have been given to General Anderson."

There is another task I may have to assign you. A most difficult task. At this time, I have ordered the rose garden, behind Buckingham palace, to be torn out. To be replaced with a machine gun range. The king, and his family will not leave London. They will fight in the streets and die with their people."

Eric is stunned. Unsure what to say and remains silent.

"You have fought in the ruined cities of France. Your courage is unquestioned. If this Britain is invaded, you will command three battalions, to protect and fight alongside the Royal family. At the last extremity, the King may ask a difficult task of you, to perform. You must obey. The King, his family will not be taken to Berlin, as a trophy of war. At the last moment, if all seems lost, you are to open this envelope, that both the King and I have signed. Keep it on your person, show no one."

Eric leaves the room, shaken, terrified as what is in the envelope, not daring to open it. As Eric leaves, a secretary brings more documents for Churchill to review.

CHAPTER 7

THE TORCH CAFÉ - SCOTT

Eric and Bill are sitting in The Torch Café, as the band plays some Jazz, with Charles playing the Sax. More soldiers and sailors entered. As Charles gives a Salute, missing a note, as he noticed Eric and Bill take a seat.

"I like this place," Bill said as he looked around, remembering when he 7 London the first time, after the first World War. "It's a good crowd and lets me listen to some American music. What a war! One moment we are planning to defend Western Civilization, Bill said. The next moment, enjoying a song and a drink."

Eric, in a philosophical mood, "It is strange. "At times it seems that I live in two worlds, two existences. I participate in a life and death struggle. When death is a instant away. Then the next moment, I am here." "You'll get over it." Bill announced.

Eric smiled, then told Bill, "Alice and Jenny are doing a short set tonight. There getting off early."

Alice walked over and smiles at Eric and Bill, as they both got up from the table. Alice gives Eric a light hug. Then turning to Bill., "I'm glad you could get some liberty. The last time we met was a bit more eventful that I would have liked."

Eric then said, "The Colonel filled me in. Hopefully this night will be less stressful."

Jenny and her brother walk to the table, as Alice introduces them. "Bill, I think you have met Jenny before. This is her brother, Scott."

"A Scotsman named Scott; I think I can handle that. Good to meet you.

Scott. You have a talented sister. I have enjoyed her performances.

"Yes Sir. She's a bright light, a wonder in my life. When on shore leave, I try to come and see her perform."

Jenny leans over and gives her brother a big hug.

Scott patted her hand, "My Mum asked me to spend some time with Jenny, when she got her first job in London."

Jenny proudly announced, "Scott found me a flat close to work. He escorted me around London, the first week I was here.

Scott smiles "Jenny. Then with a sly grin, said "Hopefully she has learned to cook a bit better. I think we had fish and chips every day." Jenny hit Scott on the shoulder. "Much better, thank you."

Scott, turning to Eric.

Good to see you, Major. I'm glad you are walking again. Alice told me you had a hard time of it.

Eric answered, with a look that bespoke of a man surprised he was still alive. "Wars are never easy. Yet many have paid a price greater than I."

Bill nods his head. "I share the same view. -I think many more will sacrifice their lives, before this war is over.

Jenny, not really listening to the conversation, gives a little jump off her seat.

"Ohhh, I have it. Jenny shrieked.

Jenny pulls out a small notebook from a purse and starts to write down some thoughts for her songs.

"A daily diary?" Bill asked as he watched Jenny furiously writing.

Scott turns and tells Bill, as Jenny continues to write.

"Jenny likes getting old songs and changing them a little, for her act. Did she do the Drunken Sailor song for you? If not, Jenny, that's my favorite."

Jenny laughed, then getting up from her seat, "Just for you, brother."

Jenny ran to the stage, talking to the band a moment and waited as they got ready. Then, hearing the first note, Jenny ran down stage, next to a table of soldiers, who cheered, realizing they had the best seats.

♪ What do you do with a drunken sailor? What do you do with a drunken sailor, what do you do with a drunken sailor, early in the morning?

Many knowing the song, the sailors being the first to join the chorus.

♪ Way hey and up she rises, way hey and up she rises, way hay and up she rises - early in the morning.

Picking up a butter from the table, to be used to pretend she is shaving a belly.

Jenny pretending, she is behind a sailor, and shaving him.

♪ "Shave his belly with a rusty razor. Shave his belly with a rusty razor. Shave his belly with a rusty razor, early in the morning."

The crowd roars its approval. The sailors, now joined by others, roar out the chorus.

♪   Way hey and up she rises, Way hey and up she rises, Way hay and up she rises early in the morning.

Jenny points to a few sailors who seem to have already drank to much.

♪   Put him in a long boat till he's sober. Put him in a long boat till he's sober. Put him in a long boat till he's sober, early in the morning.

Jenny does a quick walk around the stage, pointing at those who are not yet singing, then off to look at others, with a bounce to her step.

♪   Way hey and up she rises, Way hey and up she rises, Way hay and up she rises early in the morning.

Jenny jumps off the stage like a cat and gets behind a sailor, pretending she is shaving his belly.

The sailors start swinging their mugs of ail back, and forth as they sing.

Jenny waits for her cue and then starts running around the room and lifts her index fingers off her nipples each time the sailors sing out, "Up she rises".

♪ Way hey and up she rises, Way hey and up she rises, Way hay and up she rises, early in the morning.

The crowd once again applauds their approval and cheers wildly.

♪ Put him in bed, with the captain's daughter. Put him in bed with the captain's daughter. Put him in bed with the captain's daughter, early in the morning.

Jenny then sits down on the lap of a sailor, waiting for the first verse of "up she rises", with Scott already laughing, knowing Jenny will be looking down at each sailor's lap, as if to see if he has been aroused. Scott gives a thumbs up as Jenny looks at him, smiling getting ready to give her best performance, for her brother. The next verse, each time we hear "up she rises", Jenny comes off a sailors lap, with a look of surprise and pleasure. Knowing the whole room will go wild, then joining in the chorus.

♪ Way hey and up she rises, Way hey and up she rises, Way hay and up she rises early in the morning.

Jenny moves around the room and jabs a finger at a different sailor each time she sings "That's what" you do with a drunken sailor.

That's what you do with a drunken sailor, that's what you do with a drunken sailor, that's what you do with a drunken sailor, early in the morning.

Now the bar tenders and servers, join in with Jenny, as they stand together, joining in for the last chorus.

♪ Way hey and up she rises, Way hey and up she rises, Way hay and up she rises - early in the morning.

The last few bars of the song are played. Jenny takes her bows and goes back to the table.

" The last time, I brought my mates to watch the show. They were still talking about it next day."

"One of your mates, is a pincher. I'll be ready for the next one."

"He's not coming back."

"Good. Now, I'm almost done. Give it to the band with some old sheet music, and they'll have it ready the next time.

"What's it called, Jenny?" Eric asked.

Jenny sings out the line of the song in a bit of a sing song manner. "I wouldn't Leave My Little Wooden Hut for You!"

They all laugh for a moment and wonder about the song.

"That's an old one." Alice said.

"I have a feeling it's going to be another winner." Bill announced.

"Any hints for us, Jenny." Alice asked, knowing she might also be added into the act.

Jenny sits up a bit and take a breath. Scott, having heard it, when Jenny was practicing the song, in her flat, just smiles.

"I wouldn't leave my little wooden hut for you. I got one lover and I don't need two. I wouldn't leave my little wooden hut with

50

you. That man of arms, you see is my beau, and he seems to want to strike a blow. You'd better go."

They all laugh at Jenny's new song. Jenny puts away the notebook and Eric turns to Jenny.

Eric then informed Jenny, "I think you are right Jenny, That should scare off those men whose hands go where they do not belong."

Bill then announced, looking at Jenny, "Jenny, " Jenny, I loved the way you performed that last song. You got talent. Hollywood will be calling.

Jenny perks up and smiles, "Hollywood, like California?

Bill gave Jenny a wink, knowing of all the young women who dream of going to Hollywood and becoming actresses. "Hollywood, like California. You would be a sensation." Bill proclaimed, as Jenny beamed when Bill repeating the word, noticing how pleased Jenny was when he said, sensation, and repeated it, "A sensation."

Jenny quickly took on a serious face, ready to play any part. Then gives a little bit of the dialog from, " Gone with the Wind."

"Oh, Rhett, Where shall I go, what shall I do?"

They all laugh again as Bill smiles. "I think I'm supposed to play Clark Cable to her Vivian Leigh.

Bill pauses for a moment, getting ready to do his best Clark Cable voice.

"Frankly my dear, I don't give a damn!"

Everyone laughs again as Eric spoke up, looking at Bill, then Jenny.

"I think Jenny will need an agent if she goes to Hollywood." Eric suggested.

"There's money to be made here. I discovered you, and I will be your agent. I shall fund you for three months in Los Angeles. That should give you time for the casting calls.

Bill, then thinking for a moment, "Well, after I've finished my uh - current job."

Jenny wiggles her nose, then moved her head from side to side, smiling as if she's been hired already. Then looking down at her notebook, not wanting to lose her train of thought.

"I still have to finish my song. Just two more lines, then done."

"And I must finish buying a few things before I go back to the ship."

Scott stands up, then leans over and gives a hug to Jenny. Also giving a handshake to Eric and Bill, lightly shakes Alice's hand.

"Good to see you Major. A pleasure to meet you, Colonel."

"Same here. What ship to you sail on?"

"The HMS Hood, Sir. Were in for some repairs." Scott answered before he headed for the door.

Jenny jumped up from her seat and turned to follow Scott.

"He's not getting away from me that easy. I'll threaten him with some more home cooking. We'll go out for fish and chips.

Jenny runs after Scott, shouting, "Piggyback ride." Scott turned, laughed, and slightly bent his back, and waited for Jenny, who jumps on.

CHAPTER 8

HEADQUARTERS

The Secretary walked over to Eric. "You may go in Major."

Eric walks in and sees Gen. Anderson studying a stack of files.

"Reporting as ordered, Sir."

"At ease, Major. I think we can both relax, if only for a moment."

"Yes, Sir."

"It has not been the most joyful of Christmases, but we have survived. With thousands of our Londoners dead, parts of the city in ruin, we have paid a heavy price to stop an invasion. We must now take the offensive. Wars are not won from Bunkers or shelters." Then lifting his voice, as he hardened his tone. "But on the Battlefield."

"Yes, Sir. The men are ready to strike back. Give the Hun a bit more than they gave us."

"Our soldiers will soon have their chance. The fighting in North Africa has transformed the campaign. Our casualties have been light. Yet we have captured thousands of pieces of artillery and small weapons, tens of thousands of men."

Eric said with confidence. "It is true. Rarely in history has so much, been surrendered to so few." General Anderson said, modifying a statement famously made by Churchill.

"Roosevelt has been re-elected president. Although expected, it was a great relief to hear the results.

"His oratory skills, and commanding presence on the American stage, rally's a nation to our cause."

"The President has allocated a large portion of America's war production to England. All this within a week of his re-election. We will pay dearly, but the weapons will be ours. All our gold reserves in South Africa, are to be transferred to the US Treasury.

"We now sell and borrow against our assets. The war production plants we have built in America, have been purchased by the United States Government. The president moves quickly. Yet, we are allowed to receive all the weapons and tools of war, from those factories.

"It is hard to see how Germany could continue viewing the United States as a neutral."

General Anderson, using wit and humor, he was known for, "Madness does not respect logic." Then in a more serious voice;

Germany is not in a hurry, for war with the United States.

"My parents have been ordered to transfer to his Majesties government, all bonds, notes, and stock in American companies. It must be a terrible expenditure of funds to buy such quantities of weapons." Eric said.

We are long past the time when we had funds for the purchase of weapons, under the "cash and carry" laws. By exporting our finest goods, wool suits, Scotch, and whiskey, the confiscation of property from our citizens, we extended the time we could purchase with cash.

Eric exclaimed, "My God!"

"Those funds are now gone. We cannot now pay for even half of what we have ordered. With an invasion to be halted, cities in ruin, and starvation a possibility, his majesties government has thrown caution and frugality to the winds."

"I understand, Sir." Eric said with a smile showing at the corner of his mouth. Eric is silent for a moment, thinking of the danger.

What would have happened if we run out of money?

"Issue Bonds on a ruined city. Write a check and hope the funds are there." Remarked General Anderson, with a chuckle.

"I await orders, Sir."

"I will now also need your services as an intelligence officer, in the next few days.

"Yes, Sir."

"Are you having a good relationship with that American Colonel?"

"We both share the same views. We have become good friends."

Gen. Anderson nodded his head in approval.

Eric then offered, "Colonel Morris expects his work to be completed in the next two weeks. I believe he is satisfied that the British people have the spirit to fight on, hold on."

"Good, we grow stronger each day. Continue as you have done, with Bill Morris. He also requested that I use his first name, when off duty."

"Yes, Sir."

"We have defied the tyrant even, at his strongest. We did not flinch or waver. Now, we must start to plan the attack!"

In a loud voice, Eric shouted, "Sir, Yes, Sir."

" You are dismissed Major."

Eric salutes and leaves.

CHAPTER 9

SCOTT'S DEAD

Eric is sitting in The Torch Café, as Alice sits next to Jenny, at another table. Jenny is crying and Alice has her arm on her back for a moment, then hugging Jenny.

"He's dead Alice. I can feel it. I knew the moment it happened. I felt his soul pass through me."

"You can't be sure. He might have survived."

Jenny screams out, "NO!"

Jenny starts crying as Alice starts crying also. Bill enters The Torch Café and goes over to talk to Eric.

"She knows?"

Eric just slightly moves his head, nodding yes.

"The shell from the Bismarck must have hit the magazine. I have heard that the Hood just blew apart." Bill softly said, as he looked over at Jenny and Alice.

"I have heard the same. The Prince of Wales has also been damaged."

Bill, looking intently at Eric, I have never seen a city in mourning. There is a pale of pain, hanging over London. A quiet grief that I see on every face.

Eric and Bill just sat there, as they look towards Alice and Jenny. Alice gets a little closer to Jenny, her face right in front of Jenny.

"Jenny. Look at me. Do not let this destroy you, like it destroyed my mum. My father was killed in the first war. My mother collapsed when she heard the news.

Jenny eyes start to look at Alice, sobbing as she grasps Alice's hands.

"She finally went into a deep depression. Then into an asylum. I spent a year in an orphanage. I was nine years old. All I knew was that my father was dead, and my mum had deserted me."

Jenny hugs Alice and they both sob for themselves and for each other.

"That's it honey, let the tears flow like a river to the sea. Get it all out of you. But let the tears wash away the pain. Or the pain and grief will kill you; heart and soul, as it did my mum.

"Oh Alice."

Alice strokes Jenny's hair, then holds both her hands in hers.

"You will never forget him. He will be in your dreams and alongside of you, with his guidance, when you are in need."

Jenny seems to give a faint smile looking into Alice's eyes. As Alice continues to stroke Jenny's hair.

Bill and Eric walk over to Jenny to give their condolences.

"Jenny, I am so sorry. Scott was a good and brave man. A nation mourns for each man on the Hood. A million prayers are raised to heaven, carrying your brother with them.

"I only met Scott once. Yet, as Eric has said, in that moment, I knew him to be a good and brave man. The truth about war is that good men must die, so that evil may end."

Jenny grabs the hand of Eric and Bill and squeezes their hands and looks up.

"Thank you. Then trying to get the words out, holding back her tears, as she sobbed. " The last thing Scott said to me, the night he left, was that if he should die, I should know that he died for what he believed in."

"Jenny stands up looking at Eric and then at Bill, the tears still falling. "We must win this war. All the horror, all the death, all the cities that are now burning, must be avenged."

"I think I hear Scott in your voice. Eric said, as he placed his hand on Jenny's shoulder. Alice, also wanting to pay tribute to Scott's bravery and service. "Jenny, he stands beside you now."

"Let me take you home." Eric offered, then said, "I would like to meet your Mum."

"I think she would like that.

CHAPTER 10

ERIC PROMOTED

Eric walks into the General's office. Eric salutes.

"At ease, You are lucky you only had to deal with the PM, once in a while. Hardened men, General's come away, flustered and annoyed."

"Yes, Sir. The PM can be demanding."

"He likes you. Churchill admires men of action and courage. The Pm proved hist mettle, as an officer, and during the boar War."

General Anderson remarked. "Churchill has that you are to be given the rank of Colonel." General Anderson then handed Eric a small box.

"Thank you, Sir. Shall I remain in my current position?"

"Yes, you are to continue accompanying Colonel Morris, and American journalists. The assistance and support of the Americans is of great importance.

"Yes Sir. The PM has made that noticeably clear to me."

"Your opinion of the man. Has it changed?"

"He is still calm and determined. He supports us fully."

"Good."

"Any word on finding the Bismarck?" Eric asked.

"I have just heard that two old Biplanes, of all things, have slowed her down with torpedoes. We are trailing her now.

"Good news, Sir."

"Sending the Bismarck to Davy Jones' Locker, is the fond wish of every English man, and woman."

Eric nods his head.

"Things seem to have quieted down, for a time. The night raids have stopped." Eric remarked.

"The Germans are up to no good, when things get this quiet. They have moved hundreds of thousands, of men, back to Germany. We also have reports , that men and equipment are going East. We are not sure why. It may be to assist their Italian allies, with their attack on Greece."

"Do you think Russia will act in her sphere of influence?" Eric asked.

"It is difficult to judge what Russia's actions will be."

"Germany has a non-aggression treaty with Russia." Eric remarked.

"Non-aggression is a word, not in the vocabulary of the Nazi's. The Russians know this. It can only be seen as a momentary truce."

"The PM is the man you can ask, next time you see him." General Anderson said, with a smile.

"Churchill is not a man you question. Although at times he has confided in me, in ways that have surprised me."

"He likes men who are bold, and take action. Both of you are graduates of Sandhurst. He sees a little of himself in you. You also have the one thing he covets, but never earned, the Victoria Cross.

Eric gives a slight smile. "Thank you, Sir.

"No thanks needed. Your record speaks for itself. Continue as you have. If America should enter this war, closer contact and understanding will be critical. They will have to sacrifice, many of their sons, in this most terrible of wars. You are dismissed, Colonel."

"Yes Sir." Eric gives a snappy salute and leaves the room, smiling slightly, opening the box, to see his new insignia.

CHAPTER 11

A DRINK

The Torch Café is full of British Sailors and Soldiers. Eric has come to escort Alice home after she has finished her act. Alice comes over to sit and talk with Eric.

Alice already has her coat on.

"Hello Love. We must wait a moment. I told Jenny we could give her a lift back to her flat."

"How is she?"

"Better now. But it is still hard for her. She went back and spent some time with her mum. Her mum is also taking it hard. Scott was her only son."

"No parent can lose a child and not be torn apart." Eric said.

"Her mum is spending some time with her." Alice said. "They need each other now."

"The crowds are getting a little heavier, with the band stopping for a time to rest. The wireless providing news and music. We hear a news report that Churchill will be making a speech in Parliament the next day. The music starts again, with slow soft music.

"Ladies and Gentlemen," Charles continued looking around, seeing who the night's audience would be. "Although I fear it is more Gentlemen than ladies. The fleet must be in."

A loud laugh comes from the crowd. As Charles looks over the crowd, seeing if any one he knows is there.

"The management, being in a generous mood, an unusual occurrence, has offered a round to the table with the highest-ranking enlisted man.

Cheers from the crowd with three men standing up immediately.

Charles, now swings out his arm, "Our lovely and talented Jenny will do the honors, and pour the drinks. With my previous service in the Great War, I will identify who the highest-ranking enlisted man is. If there is a tie, then the longest serving man wins."

Cheers as the crowd starts to see Charles going from table to table. One man stands up as Charles approaches.

Why you Sir. I think you are the man I'm looking for. State your name and rank.

"Mark Richard, Chief Petty Officer.

"A brave soul indeed. Especially when you have a Warrant Officer sitting behind you." Charles said.

The crowd laughs again. As the Warrant Officer takes a bow and holds his empty glass.

The chief Petty officer calls out.

"Yes but is he an enlisted man or an officer."

Laughter from the crowd.

"Before I get into that discussion. I think I have a solution. I believe our sweet Jenny can be talked into pouring drinks for both tables".

Jenny smiles and gives a quick curtsy, then holds up the bottle. A cheer goes up from the crowd. Jenny runs over and pours drinks for both tables.

"Now, my fine friends, a drink for the most important job in the service. Any cooks here? Without them you would all starve."

Some laughter from the crowd, as a few men point out the cook.

"I hold that illustrious position. I'll take a drink, and the bottle - if I may. Marinate my lamb chops, if you will."

Another man shouts out, "Yes, and I could use a bottle for my bath."

More laughs from the crowd, with Eric and Bill joining in the laughter.

"Now, Now, Gentleman, rations are in force. We only have a limited supply. Jenny, a drink for that fine fellow.

Jenny runs over and pours a drink for the cook and then goes back onto the stage with Charles.

Charles announces, "Jenny has a last song to sing, this night. She is accepting requests from the audience."

Men jump up and start shouting out songs they want to hear. Jenny turns around and listens to the crowd yelling out their requests.

"Jenny, Jenny, let's hear the Drunken sailor song." Jenny laughs, sticks out her tongue and touches her nipples, knowing that many of the men have seen her perform that song many times. The crowd laughs.

"I've already done that song - a lot!"

Something new, Jenny. Something new.

"Jenny looks delighted at the request.

"I have just finished a new song. I am still practicing.

"Ah, go on Jenny. We are the kindest group of sailors, you will find."

Another sailor yelling out, "Before the liquor hits."

The crowd screams its laughter as they know they can become a unruly group of sailors.

Jenny signals the band, who have returned to their seats and start to play the song that Jenny has practiced with them. The music starts.

♪   Once, on this Island, there dwelt, a dark eyed maiden.

Jenny passes her fingers by her eyes.

♪   Who lived all alone. In a little log hut, where she reigned as a queen.

Jenny makes a majestic move as if nodding her head to her subjects and puts on a fake crown.

♪   Till one day a stranger appeared on the scene. And said, "My sweet, why waste your time, in this awful clime?"

Jenny opens her palm, as if to see if it is raining.

♪   Oh, come with me, my pretty Maiden, he said to me.

The wireless comes alive as a man turns up the sound. A few men start to listen.

"This is the BBC. We have a special announcement to make."

Jenny stops for a moment and the band also stops playing the song. All now turn towards the wireless, to listen. What is such important news, that called for an interruption of the normal broadcast.

"We have been informed by the Prime Minister's office, that the Bismarck has been sent to the bottom of the sea. Further reports will follow."

A great shout goes up from the crowd as men and women cheer. Jenny looks at the band and immediately jumps on a chair with one foot on the table.

Jenny now starts to sing, Hail Britannia with joy, tears, fury, and a full release from the pain; all coming out of her at the same time. She starts to sing, with the band joining as Jenny voices the first words.

♪ Rule Britannia, Britannia rules the waves,
never, never, never, shall we be slaves.

All the crowd of Sailors join in the verse once again as Jenny leads.

♪ Rule Britannia, Britannia rules the waves,
never, never, never, shall we be slaves.

I wild cheer goes up as Jenny glories in the shouts of her compatriots, then turns away to hide the tears.

Alice, seeing Jenny, "Let's go get her."

Alice and Eric go to meet Jenny, with tears in both their eyes, Alice, and Jenny hug each other. "Jenny, I will never forget this night."

"Thank you. It was for them, and Scott." Eric, having held back, allowing them to bond, as only women can, now moves along side Alice and Jenny.

Eric now speaking up, "Jenny, Let me take you home. If Possible, I would love to meet your mother."

"I think she would like that."

Eric opens the door for Jenny and Alice, with the Sign, "The Torch Café" above the door, blinking as they left.

CHAPTER 12

RUSSIA ATTACKED

Eric walks into General Anderson's office, as uniformed men and women, almost running out. All is haste and movement. An old man, a general, is seen running out.

"I would think that you have heard the news." General Anderson asked, knowing that if he had not, something was wrong.

Eric immediately responded "Yes Sir. The Germans have attacked Russia. A stunning move by Herr Hitler.

"It only confirms my belief that he is mad. To turn his back to a rearmed Britain, is a strategic blunder. Yet, all the better for us."

"Yes, Sir."

"We do not care if we plunge the knife into his wicked heart or in his back. It will serve the same end."

"Yes, Sir. I fully agree."

"We have beaten the Germans out of the daylight, and night skies of England, when we stood alone. We are not alone now." General Anderson said, almost rumbling the words .

"Russia is a powerful nation, with a large military. The great Russian Bear will fight with tooth and claw, for the very life of Mother Russia is now in the balance.

"If I might ask, Sir. Have we any reports from the battlefield?"

"We advised Stalin of an imminent attack by Germany. Stalin seems not to have heeded our warnings. The Germans have made swift advances and have broken the initial Russian lines of defense.

Most of Russia's air force has been destroyed on the ground."

A woman runs in and looks at Eric, then drops papers on the General's desk. He stopped for a moment and gives the documents a quick read.

General Anderson looked up. "No word from Stalin to our offer of mutual assistance. A strange time for a man to go mute."

"I would think that he is rallying Russia's military forces," Eric said.

"I should hope so. Eric, I will be sending you to Russia, with a group of other military officers. You're to evaluate what can be done to help Russia. This request is coming from the top, Churchill"

"Yes, Sir."

General Anderson saw a slight smile on Eric's face.

"Yes, I know. It is a strange set of affairs. Churchill has spent twenty years denouncing Communism, and now, I am asking you to do all you can to help, the largest communist nation in the world. "The enemy of my enemy, is my friend."

"I have heard it said that war makes strange bed fellows." Eric slyly said.

"It does indeed." General Anderson got up and moved towards a map in his office. Pointing to it, "Three to four army groups have attacked the Soviet Union. With Hitler's jackal, Mussolini, providing all the support he can.

"There seems to be no end to treachery and betrayal by Hitler."

"With a treaty of non-aggression in place, no warming given, no ultimatum, no declaration of war. This monster of madness, with a lust for blood and plunder, now marches into Russia."

General Anderson went back to his seat and grabs a cigar. Holding it in his hand, he offers it to Eric, who immediately took it.

"Thank you, Sir." Eric places it in his coat pocket."

"It came from Churchill's desk. The Canadians and Americans are sending boxes of Cuban cigars to the Prime Minister."

Pausing for a minute, "If allowed, this Nazi war machine will not stop with Russia, but will eventually attack India, then join with Japan, in their attack against China."

"There is no limit to the carnage and ruin that the Germans would inflect on soldiers and civilians. I have seen it." Eric grimly said.

"You know more than most, that Nazi Germany cannot be appeased, or negotiated with. There will be no pirates parley between Stalin and Hitler. Only the complete destruction of Hitler's Germany can be Russia and England's goal." General Anderson said.

Eric comes to attention as he seems to know that General Anderson is ready to give him his orders.

"You will express to the Russian officers you meet, Churchill's hatred and disdain for Nazi Germany. You have met the Prime Minister and know his thinking. Churchill is considering a trip to Russia; you may be laying the groundwork."

"It will be my pleasure, Sir. "

"You will tell them, that it is the will of this land, and the Commonwealth, that never, never shall we negotiate with.

That Germany's utter ruin is our only goal."

"Yes, Sir. I shall express the Prime Minister's views as forcefully as I can."

"Inform the Russians that we shall increase our bombings of Germany each month. Give to the Hun the same taste of misery that they have given to Poland, France, England, and now Russia.

In war, it is shear folly to hold back one's mightiest blows. Herr Hitler shall receive a continuous rain of bombs and blows.

"Yes Sir. It will be a pleasure to utter such words."

How are your discussions and tours with Colonel Morris proceeding?

"Very well, Sir. Colonel Morris seems to have gathered all the material and information he needs. He still stands steadfast with our cause."

"Good, I have learned more about Colonel Morris, from the American Ambassador. He is well known in the political circles of the President's party. His views are listened to by the President. He is a Banister, who left a very lucrative law practice, to put on an American uniform, expecting war with Japan or Germany."

"I believe that I have developed a good relationship with Colonel Morris. I like the man. He has seen the face of war and never wants to see it in his own homeland. He would rather fight the Nazi's in Europe, than in the streets of New York or Chicago.

"That is also my opinion of Colonel Morris. He is a man of intelligence, courage, and action."

"He feels himself now part of the struggle. I think that Colonel Morris would advise for war with Germany."

"Very good. The passing of the lend lease Act has been of immense help to us. The arsenal of Democracy that is America, when put to the test, is almost limitless in its industrial capacity, resources."

"So, the Americans will continue to extend credit to us?"

General Anderson smiled, trying to hold back a chuckled, a laugh. "We now have much better terms. The Americans have tossed out the book of accounts. There are no provisions for war supplies to be paid for! The defeat of Hitler, and the defense of North America has been declared to be of vital interest to the great Republic and more important than dollars.

"A much better deal. Sir. When do you expect that I will depart?

"Soon, Colonel, soon.

"Have another cigar."

Eric takes it. "Thank you, sir. A cigar from Churchill's desk! I shall send it to my father. He smokes cigars. Although I doubt that he will ever smoke this one."

"You are dismissed, Colonel."

CHAPTER 13

DINNER WITH BILL

Alice and Eric are in Alice's flat as Bill knocks at the door and Eric opens it.

"Just in time. Alice has prepared the dinner and I have been able to find fresh garden vegetables."

"Then it shall be a feast. I was able to talk the Embassy supply officer into providing some additional provisions. A secret mission I told him."

"You Didn't." Alice looked at Bill for a moment, wondering what he had told him.

"Well, my reasons for being in England are confidential. That could be considered secret. And my latest assigned task is to enjoy my last few days in London; a mission I have accepted.

"Who would have assigned you such a lovely job?

"The War Department. Things seem to be heating up in Washington. I have been told to expect fourteen-to-sixteen-hour workdays when I get back."

Eric, knowing the rigors of war, days without sleep, simply said, "Please enjoy your last few days in London."

"Yes, please." Alice repeated. Bill smiles and hands his bag to Alice as she reaches out to receive it.

"So, you are going back?"

"I have finished my discussions with your military, and Washington is starting to sound like an impatient bride. They want an oral presentation for the report I had written and sent.

"I think you'll do fine, Alice said."

"Thank you, Alice. I hope the joint chiefs of Staff are as pleasant and approving as you.

"Any word on your next assignment?" Eric asked.

"I have been placed in intelligence, and analysis.

Bill is silent for a moment. "Japan is starting to make noises in the Pacific. Their attack on China, that we denounced, annoyed them. Seems the Japanese do not like our embargo of raw materials. There is uncertainty in both military and Political circles as to what they might do."

"Gentleman, I understand that military men will speak of war, at such times as these. Yet we only have a few hours together. I will request more pleasant conversation in a little while."

Bill laughed, "We hear and obey, as Eric gave Alice a salute. Eric moved towards the radio, "I think we can change the channel to some music and turn off the radio. An evening without news, good or bad, is needed by all.

Alice then said, "Now, for a night of music and pleasant conversation.

"A welcome change." As Bill readily agreed.

Alice pours some tea and serves plates with rolls.

"Bill, we know so little about you. Where do you call home?" Alice asked as she brought some sugar to the table.

A small town in Upstate New York. Mostly woodland, pastures and farms. The Autumn colors are a wonder to behold. It's funny, I used to think we were city boys, not farm boys; just because we lived in a town of six hundred people.

"Then you learned what a city was." Alice said.

"Yes, a tour of New York and Boston was an awakening."

"A surprise I would imagine." Eric offered, as he took a sip of tea.

"The people, the crowds, the noise; the Skyscrapers reaching up to the heavens. Yes, a great surprise when you are nine years old." "Still think you're a city boy?" Alice asked.

"Well, not a city boy and not a farm boy. A boy who grew to be a man, wanting to see and explore the world.

"None of the country boy seems to be there anymore."

Oh, he's still there. He still knows to get up before sun rise.

"And where did that county boy learn to dance?" "A few lessons from my sister, so that I would not step on the toes of her girlfriends, and a dance club in college, so that I might enjoy the company of the fairer sex."

"A worthwhile and useful skill. Women can dance the night away."

Alice looks at Eric and realizes that her words have upset him. Alice also sees that Bill is a little uncomfortable with her statement. Alice pats Eric on the hand. "Then there are women who have found the man whom they would share their lives with."

"Thank you love. With time, I will glide you across the dance floor again."

"With time, this war will be over, and I will never let you leave me."

"Well, at least let me earn my place at the table with a few goodies. I had a grandfather who worked the farm and believed if you did not do an honest day's labor, or if you did not bring something to the table, you had no right to sit at the table.

"A hard man. Eric said.

"Yes, but an honest hard-working man. That is how the men of that generation thought. Also knowing that the English are rationed, two ounces of butter and tea per person, I was able to work a deal with a fellow officer, so that I might contribute to the table.

Alice and Eric nodded their heads, as Alice becoming curious, grabbed the bag and looked inside. With rations holding everyone to their diet, I think we might find some surprises in this Bag.

"Allow me," Bill said, "I was informed that these were the rarest of prizes. Since he wished to use my staff car to take out a certain English Lady, he agreed to part with them.

"California wine, you're joking." Alice exclaimed, as Bill continued pulling out more items.

"Fresh apples and oranges. I have not seen these in two years." Eric mused for a moment; I shall tell myself this is my welcome home party."

Alice laughed, and throw out her hands at the bounty, "A treasure trove."

"It was only a matter of trading my staff car to the supply officer, for an evening."

"A find fellow indeed." Eric cheered.

"Let me find a bottle opener." As Alice got up and picked one from the drawer. Alice gives the bottle opener to Eric, who opens, and pours each a glass.

They all raise their glasses.

"To enjoy the company of friends, and pleasant conversation, is the greatest of pleas, Bill offered as his toast. " Cheers."

"To all those brave men who fight the Nazi's. To our French allies, Liberty, Equality, Futurity. Cheers." Eric said, as he offered the next toast." Eric showing some emotion, remembering the French soldiers he fought with, who he saw fall."

Bill, know he still had a lot to do that night, "I must ask your leave. I meet with my staff in the morning, and then start to pack."

"It has been a pleasure having you here." Alice said. then lifting the bottle of wine, " Thank you for Christmas in October."

Bill stands up and grabs his hat and coat, off a chair by the door.

"Thank you for such a fine dinner, and a pleasant evening. These are the days you remember. Oh, yes, this is for Jenny."

"Some more Chocolate?"

"Jenny mentioned to me how much she loves Chocolate," Bill said, as he pulled them out of his coat pocket, and handed them to Alice.

"I am sure. Jenny mentions to every American she meets; how much she loves Chocolate!"

Bill smiles. "Once again, thank you ."

"Our pleasure." Eric and Alice said.

"We will see each other again." Eric said as he extended his hand, "I am sure of it."

Eric and Bill shake hands and Bill lifts up Alice's hand and kisses it.

"Something I learned in Paris."

Alice smiles and Eric opens the door for Bill to leave and closes the door.

"That's a good fellow."

"He has that old kind of chivalry in him." "Yes, I have seen that in some of the Americans."

"Eric motions to the sofa as he and Alice take a seat, with Eric putting down the wine bottle.

"It would be a shame to forget about that bottle of wine and not use it."

"I have a solution. The necessities of war require that we enjoy the "Rest,and Recreation." Eric pours a glass of wine into Alice's glass, and some more into his glass.

"I shall have to send an anonymous letter to the American embassy, thanking them."

Eric pauses for a moment and lays down his glass. "Alice there is something I did want to tell you."

"If it is about the war, I will not hear it. I wish for a quiet evening, in your arms. Morning comes soon enough."

"Then I shall make your wishes come true." Eric softly said.

CHAPTER 14

WAR WITH JAPAN

It is late in the evening, and the Torch Café is filled with couples, soldiers, and sailors.

Eric and Alice are sitting at a table in the middle of the room. Alice turns to Eric that "Jenny's doing a new song tonight. I've been watching the rehearsals. It's funny."

"From Jenny, that's easy to believe."

"Jenny got a standing ovation from the band the first time they practiced the song."

"From those old hands, that's a compliment."

"I think it's going to be the first song she performs tonight."

Charles walks onto the stage, as the band starts to get ready.

"Ladies and Gentlemen, we have a fine show for you tonight. A vaudevillian variety show, with a little bit of old and a little bit of new."

The crowd cheers as Jenny walks onto the stage and stands next to Charles.

"Now, for that songstress you're all cheering for, our poet in residence, Jenny of the golden hair. Take a bow, Jenny."

Cheers once again from the crowd. Jenny smiles and puts her finger under her chin and makes a little curtsy.

"Thank you! Your all so very kind. This is a song I have been practicing with the band and you will now hear its first performance. The song is titled. 'There's a Little Bit of Bad in Every Good Little

Girl.' " laughter and cheers greet Jenny for the new song.

Charles walks over to the band and Jenny bows again as the crowd cheers her on for her first performance. The band starts the song as Jenny waits a few moments for her cue.

♪ "Nobody ever dances with the good girls."

Jenny takes on a sad face.

♪ "It makes the goods girls so sad."

Jenny starts to brighten up and smiles a little wicked little smile.

♪ "All the men want to dance with the bad girls,"
  Jenny said with a knowing face.
  "It makes the bad girls so glad."
  "But when you've been around those girls once
  or twice, you can't tell the naughty from the
  nice."

The crowd laughs and cheers Jenny on.

♪ "There's a little bit of bad in every good little
  girl. They're not to blame. Mother Eve was
  just the same. Didn't she eat the apple,

Jenny pretended to bite into an apple,

♪ "and raised Cain?"

Jenny gives a wicked little smile. Then starts to skip around the stage, singing as she goes.

♪   "There's a little bit of bad in every good little girl. Their not to blame, their all the same."

The crowd cheers as Jenny gives a "come hither look" , an inviting smile.

♪   "I know a preacher's daughter, who likes her gin - and never touches water. Why bother?"

The crowd cheers as Jenny gives a look of a women a little drunk and silly.

♪   "There's a little bit of bad in every good little girl. They're not to blame, their all the same."

Jenny points to a few women in the audience as they smile at her and Jenny then points at herself and curtseys again.

♪   "Though they seem like angels in a dream, Jenny gives a sweet angelic look, "When you get them behind a door, its a very different scene. They'll be both naughty and nice, and now you'll have to think it over twice."

In the final chorus Jenny makes faces that go from good girl to bad girl.

"There's a little bit of bad in every good little girl. Their not to blame, there all the same. There's a little bit of bad in every good little girl. Their not to blame, mother nature made all the creatures the same."

The song stops and Jenny just stands there, with that wicked smile. The crowd cheers.

Charlies shouts out, "Jenny, come on back and take a few more bows."

Jenny comes back and takes a few bows.

"We still have a night of entertainment and laughter. Please enjoy the company of lovers and friends." Charles said.

Jenny then said, "It's fine, if you order a wee bit more wine."

Jenny joins Eric.

"Jenny, that was wonderful. I'm starting to think that I should be the opening act and you're the closer."

"I'm the comedy act and you're the closer. You sing like a nightingale."

Alice smiles and gives Jenny a little hug.

"Just loved it. That's the kind of morale booster our men need. Let's them escape this war for a few hours."

"Thank you. Seeing the smiles on their faces and hearing their laughter, pleases me beyond words."

Eric pulls out the chair as Jenny sits down.

Eric asked Jenny, "What can I order you?"

"Allow me, it's free if I order it."

Eric laughs for a moment and Alice nods her head, agreeing with Jenny.

"One of our benefits."

"I bow to your superior wisdom."

Jenny turns and waves to one of the waiters and holds up her hand as if holding up a drink. The waiter, with a nod, and a knowing look, goes to the bar, to get what Jenny wants.

"A mind reader?" Eric asked.

"I order the same thing every time."

Two sailors walk into The Torch Café, and go talk to some of the other sailors. There seems to be interest and excitement on their faces and in their voices. Eric seems to notice, as Alice and Jenny continue to talk.

"There seems to be some excitement tonight."

Eric nods his head in the direction of the sailors talking. Alice and Jenny look at all the crowd starting to talk, getting excited.

"Ladies, there is a war going on."

Alice and Jenny see a stern and serious look on Eric and quiet down.

"Yes, Eric." Alice said.

The time is Sunday at 8:00 pm. Jenny nods her head and looks a little contrite. A man comes on stage and talks to Charles, who is still standing next to an open mic. We hear Charles gasp in a loud voice.

"My God!"

Eric stands up, now knowing that something very important has happened. Charles moves closer to the mic.

"I have just been informed that the Japanese have attacked the Americans in Hawaii. Their naval base at Pearl Harbor. Ships have been sunk, thousands have been killed."

Eric stands and shouts out, "Are you sure?"

The sailor who has informed Charles answers Eric.

"Yes, Sir. It has been broadcast on the Wireless for the last ten minutes. Churchill will be addressing the House of Commons. He is expected to declare war against Japan."

"My God!"

Alice looks around and sees many looking stunned, as the crowd continuing to talk, with a few officers starting to leave.

"What does it mean Eric?" Alice asks.

"It means that the Americans are now in this war, up to the neck and in to the death. We now have a world at war."

Alice and Jenny look surprised at Eric's words and hardened face, but immediately understand.

"We have a bases in Singapore, and in Australia. Scott visited them when he was in the Pacific."

"I would expect the Japanese to attack our military forces in the Pacific. If they have not already done so." Eric stops for a moment, knowing that two ships the Repulse and the Prince of Wales have been sent to Singapore, without air support.

Charles walks over to Eric, Alice, and Jenny. A look of stunned surprise still on his face. Charles. in a dead pan voice, "As the Americans would say, It's a different ball game!"

Eric nods his head in complete agreement, as Charles sits down at the table.

"The Americans will react with an absolute fury. I know them. It is a mighty nation, with a hundred and thirty million people. An industrial base that is unequaled."

Alice, remembering her previous conversation with Charles, " , you once told me you traveled through America."

"Yes, for three years. It was after the first great war. I had served in France, and had a chance to listen to American music, especially Jazz. I had to visit that nation and learn more about the music and the people."

"What was it like?" Jenny asked.

"First, I traveled to New Orleans, then up the Mississippi by bus, listening at Jazz clubs, small bars and café's. Meeting Americans on the streets, in nightclubs and later, visiting in their homes."

"Then you know the Americans!"

"I know them. They still have a strong work ethic, and a willingness to fight when provoked."

"When they marshal their forces, the Japanese will be God struck by what has hit them. The Americans will have no mercy on the Japanese, after such a surprise attack.

"I agree. Germany has a defense treaty with Japan. We shall have to see if the Germans will be so foolish as to declare war against the United States."

"There is neither wit nor wisdom in Herr Hitler. I believe he will declare war against the United States."

"Eric sees a few more officers leaving."

"Please excuse me. I will need to call in and see if I need to report for duty."

"Please use the phone in my office." Charles offered.

Eric leaves and goes up the steps and behind the stage curtain.

"I did not know you sent so much time there."

"Three years. I went with my clarinet and my Sax, and played at dance halls, county fairs, night clubs and baseball games. If you wanted to stay working as a musician in America, you learned every kind of music. Every region was different."

Eric comes back into the room and stands next to Alice.

"Well, at least one last night to enjoy good company. I report early tomorrow. I think it will be some time before I am given another three-day leave."

"We should go home. There are arms that want to hold me, kisses I long for."

CHAPTER 15

———

A SECOND FRONT

Gen. Anderson's secretary looks into his office to see if he has finished reading his reports.

"You may go in, Colonel."

General Anderson. Placing down the phone, motioned to Eric, "Have a seat Colonel, there is much to discuss. We are now at war with Japan."

"Yes, Sir. I listened to Churchill's speech in the House of Commons."

"The PM had previously warned the Japanese that any attack upon the United States would bring a declaration of war from this United Kingdom. A declaration of war, was declared by Churchill, even before the US Congress could meet."

"It was a fine speech. All the issues that his Majesties government had considered, before war with Japan was declared, were given.

"All though I must say, it would have been difficult not to declare war against Japan, after their attack against our forces in Malaya, hours after Pearl Harbor." Gen. Anderson looked at Eric for a moment, to see how Eric would react.

"It does simplify things." Eric suggested.

"It does indeed. The Japanese have brought the Americans into this war. Their military has made a fatal mistake. They will be ground to dust."

"It was reckless audacity to attack the Americans on a Sunday, in such a brutal and treacherous manner."

"It has stunned even those of us who have been at the center of the storm. The PM was at Chequers, with the American Ambassador. I have heard they both leaped to their feet upon hearing the news."

"I reacted in the same manner, Sir. It seemed so improbable that the Japanese would take such action."

"The insane ambition and ceaseless appetite of nations has made many act reckless, beyond measure. It is a lesson history has taught us. Hitler's madness has infected the Japanese military and its people. After watching the German's obtain new possessions', the new password on the streets of Tokyo, is "Don't miss the Bus.""

Eric, trying to hide a smile, "Now, Germany has declared war against the United States."

"Yes Colonel, it simplifies things. To have Russia, China and now the United States at our side, bonded together in this great struggle, makes victory a certainty. This Island nation will not feel the yoke or lash."

"I agree. The free peoples of the world are many times the power and population of Germany, Italy, and Japan. I can see no manner or means in which the Axis powers could win."

"Exactly so. I would not lessen the dangers or gravity that we now face in the Pacific. We must expect that Japan will continue to assault our interests. They may attempt an invasion of Australia, New Zealand or even India."

"I have heard that the Australians are demanding the return of their soldiers, from North Africa.

General Anderson with a stern, and yet uncertain face, pauses for a moment, before answering. "It is true. The Australian Prime Minister has written to their newspapers, stating that Australia would demand the return of its soldiers, and would now rely on the United States for its defense."

"Such a statement could not come at a worse time."

"It is true, but more pressing issues must be dealt with. We have had preliminary discussions with the Americans. We have agreed to form a joint operations command."

Gen. Anderson now spoke in a loud and more forceful tone.

"The U-boats are already sinking ships just miles away from New York. I have been surprised by the lack of planning, to protect shipping along the coasts of North America."

"Yes, Sir, which surprised me also."

"In the future, this England shall find itself host to an armada of ships, men and supplies."

"It is as I would expect." Eric said.

"That American you briefed and whom you accompanied."

"Colonel Morris?"

"General Morris. He was promoted to a two-star General within days of Japan's attack on Hawaii. He will be returning with the first group of military officers."

"Yes, Sir. We parted as good friends. I *would expect to continue that friendship.*"

"Good! He should be here in a few hours. You are once again to be assigned to the group of officers who will meet with the Americans, in the formation of the joint command."

" Sir, one question. Shall we continue to defer to the Americans?"

"No, not any more. The Americans are in this war, with all their life blood committed to this great struggle. We argue for our own interests now."

With a quick, but fleeting smile, "Yes, Sir."

"Colonel, that envelope you carry." Eric stands silent. "Yes, I am aware of its existence. There are only four of us who are aware of its existence. It is to be, returned to the office of the Prime Minster. To be included, in his private papers."

"Yes Sir. It is a burden that I would freely give up."

"You are dismissed Colonel. Be back in two hours."

"Yes, Sir." Eric gives a snappy salute and leaves.

CHAPTER 16

BILL'S BACK

General Anderson is seated and talking to General Morris, as Eric walks in. They both stand, With Bill immediately offering his hand.

"Colonel, I am sure you remember General Morris."

"Colonel, good to see you."

"General, glad to welcome you back to England. When things are not so desperate."

"We have turned the corner on the Fascists. Russia and Ukraine fight on." Bill said with evident pleasure.

Eric replied, "The battle for the Atlantic, has been won. The launching of planes from modified ships, to find the U-Boats, has turned the tide.

"Yes, but at a prohibitive cost, for a time." Bill said.

"Eric nods his head and gives a knowing look. "I followed the numbers, the tonnage lost. For a time, I wondered if a solution would be found."

"I also wondered." Bill responded. "From the North Cape to the Pyrenees, the U-boats were being unleashed. With twenty U-boats being built each month, it was a touch and go situation. The newspapers were instructed to no longer report on the ships sunk."

"With our ports at Clyde, Mersey and Bristol damaged from bombing raids, the Channel became a war zone. Especially dangerous, when near the Channel Islands, now occupied by the Germans."

Neither Eric nor Bill or Eric, wanting to acknowledge that English land was occupied. Eric then said, "Our shipments were reduced by half."

"You are fortunate to have Churchill at such a time. As we are to have Roosevelt. Churchill's speech on the battle for the Atlantic, rallied Americans, as I am sure it rallied your people."

"It focused the nation and the Navy, on the peril. Just before the wolf packs started to strike."

"It was air power that finally made the difference. Once we could catapult fighter planes from modified cargo ships, we were able to find, and attacked their U-Boats."

"I was at the war department when final agreement was reached for the United States to take over the protection of Iceland, insuring air support and protection of the convoys. An assignment that I relished." Bill said.

"We can breathe now. I had been informed that you would be arriving with the group of Americans, to formation of the joint command." Eric said.

"That was my understanding. My orders were changed. Not the first time in this man's army. I was kept in Washington, to help plan the initial assaults on Japanese held Islands. The Island-hopping Campaign."

Eric nodded his head.

" We learned some hard lessons at Tarawa, and Guadalcanal."

"Hard fought battles, indeed. I followed the campaigns in our daily briefings. After the fall of our Pacific bases, the imprisonment of our soldiers at Singapore, it became of utmost importance."

"I understand that you are now to serve with the joint command?" Eric said.

"Yes. I was glad to hear that you are also on the joint operations command. My fellow officers have spoken highly of your abilities and foresight."

"Thank you, General Morris."

Bill smiles and wants Eric to call him Bill but will not make such a request in front of others.

"There are a lot of questions I would like to ask you."

"Gentlemen, please feel free to use my office. I do have another meeting that I must attend within the hour."

"Thank you, I appreciate that." Bill answered."

Gen. Anderson leaves the office and both Eric and Bill sit down.

"Good to see you, Eric. You are walking much better."

"It took about four months after you left, before I started walking without a cane. I can truly say *I danced with Alice, if not the whole night, at least an hour.*"

"Good to hear. How is Alice and Jenny?"

"They are both doing well."

" The Torch Café. Still going strong?"

"They fill the house. But the show is different. Charles has changed the act. With so many Americans coming, he wanted to appeal to everyone in the audience."

"That's good. Nothing like some hometown music to make those boys feel comfortable. For many of them, military service is the first time they've been more than 50 miles from their homes."

"I found that out. I had a friendly conversation with an American soldier. He said he had heard rumors that his company might be stationed in Dover. He could not understand why they would send him to the state of Delaware." Bill gave a hearty laugh.

"I can understand the confusion. I was myself surprised by how many cities in the United States were named after English towns and cities. Be careful if you tell them they are being stationed in Birmingham, Cambridge, York, Oxford, or Liverpool. They may think you are sending them home."

Eric smiles for a moment.

"I was once that kid. Knowing nothing, of the world. Yet, every one of them has my respect and admiration." Bill said, with pride on his face.

"Here, here. That is certain." Eric said. "Our men and women, know they fight for America, but know they also fight for English land and English liberty."

"All those men, in their own way and for their own reasons, have answered the battle cry of Freedom. I have been proud to serve with them, and I am willing to die alongside of them." Bill said, with a certainty that no one would question.

A moment of silence grips both Bill and Eric. They both know the consequences of war for their men and for themselves.

"Well said, General. We share those sentiments."

"Eric, I know we will be working together, but in private, amongst friends, call me Bill."

"Thank you, Sir. It's a pleasure to know you as a friend."

"Same here. Now tell me about The Torch Café. I missed it when I was across the pond."

"Charles, you have met him?"

"Yes, I remember him."

"He spent three years traveling throughout the United Sates. He is familiar with Jazz, the big band sound, Souza marches and country music. His command of American regional dialects has surprised everyone."

"That I must hear." Bill said.

"I am sure you will. I told Alice and Jenny you had returned. They have invited you to see their new show."

"A pleasure. Can Charles *yodel those country songs?*"

"Better than any cowboy you ever heard."

Bill laughs again and smiles at Eric.

"There's still that country boy in me. Charles might find a General yodeling alongside of him."

"You might want to wear your civilian clothes."

"Yes, I will consider it. But as a General, I could command a standing ovation."

"As long as it's not louder that the applause Alice and Jenny receive.

I could not promise you a return visit if that were not the case."

"Understood. How have my fellow Americans been behaving themselves? You have a few thousand walking around now. A lot more coming."

"Mostly, they've been behaving themselves. There has been some friction and some envy. We have been on rations for some years.

We work and fight on empty stomachs."

"Women trouble. Is that where this discussion is going?"

"Not a surprise is it! Eric responded.

"Not at all. Saw it in the first great war. When tens of thousands of young men on leave, started to look for women.

"Our boys compete with nylon stockings, juice, candies, cigarettes and a wealth of other items. Not to mention the money to take a woman out for an evening. I have heard a few of our Tommies saying, that the Americans are overpaid, over sexed, and over here."

"I can see the problem."

"There is also a certain swagger and friendly charm that seems to be very appealing to our women."

"Must be all those American movies, you English watch."

Eric smiles and laughed. "Yes, that could be true. Compared to Americans, our men are shy.

"I cannot say our men are shy. I have already given approval for several Americans to marry English women, and I have only been at my duty station for three days. Not much I could do, when two of them told me she was giving birth in a three weeks."

"Hundreds have already married."

"I think it will be in the tens of thousands before this war is over. You will need a ship to carry them to America. Should be interesting when they get to Europe. It would not be the same language." Eric said, as he was fluent in French.

"There is a language to love all its own. A smile is hello. A raised bottle of wine means please join me. A kiss is universal in all its implications."

"You may be right."

"It worked for me."

"Our boys will have to learn to accept the current situation. Although I have overheard one man state that there was a new brand of knickers - "One Yank and they're off."

Bill roars in laughter. And Eric smiles and joins in with the laughter.

"Eric, my friend. There are lots of American women who love an English accent. Your men would find very friendly ladies if they should ever visit the States."

"As one might say, A tit for a tat." Eric said, with a smile.

Bill roars again in laughter as Eric smiles. "You've been hanging around to many Americans. Your English sense of humor is changing."

"You Americans have a way of being direct in a very funny way. I learned that again when I read the pamphlets you hand out to your soldiers, and sailors as to English manners and customs."

Eric looks up to the sky, as if trying to remember the words.

"Let me see if I remember. Never criticize the King. It's impolite to criticize your hosts... Bill completed the sentence.

"And militarily stupid to criticize your allies. I know that line by heart. I read it to the men who have been assigned to my office."

Eric continues, "Don't be a showoff. Do not complain about the Sun not coming out. That is just the way it is. The English cannot make a good cup of coffee. Americans cannot make a good cup of tea. It's an even swap!"

Eric, taking a quick glance at the clock on the wall, knowing that he had promised to take Alice top The Torch Café. "Then, tomorrow, at the Torch Café?"

Can't wait." Bill said.

———

CHAPTER 17

CHARLES

The Torch Café is filled with American and English soldiers and sailors. Charles looks out at the crowd and starts to address everyone.

His gray suit, with his Gray' polished shoe's, gathering himself, and collecting a deep breath, "Ladies and Gentlemen, sailors and soldiers, men of the crown and men of America, welcome to the Torch Café. We have a night of entertainment."

A warm cheer from the crowd, with Charles lifting his trumpet.

"Musicians, who know the popular songs you adore. Comedians who will keep you laughing on the floor. Songbirds for every season."

"Now, for the talented and lovely nightingales of the evening, Alice Evens and Jenny MacDonald.

Alice walks out and takes a bow as the crowd roars in appreciation for Alice. Then Jenny walks out.

"Our lovely Jenny. To show our American friends, that comedy still rules in 'Merry Old England'."

With an air of gaiety, and a smile that greets all, Jenny turns to wave. Both Alice and Jenny leave the stage.

Eric and Bill enter the Torch Café and move through the crowd to a table reserved for them. Charles comes over and greets Eric and Bill.

"Hello. Glad your back, General, Eric." It's good to be back." Bill said.

"A much better mood in London now. A smile comes easy." said Charles, with a relaxed face.

Bill, agreeing," The currents now moves in our direction. There are hard battles to be fought, but victory is assured."

"Charles, please join us." Eric asked, "Charles walked up.

Charles hesitates a moment, then drops into a chair. "Thank you. I've been on my feet all day. They could use a rest. Age has a way of slowing you down."

Bill inquired, after Charles had gathered his breath. "Eric tells me you are performing more American music."

"Dare you ask why?" Charles looks around at all the Americans.

"It's understandable." Bill agreed.

"When the crowd changes, the music must also change. It's the best way to stay in business."

Charles spreads out his arms.

"We perform everything, Jazz, Broadway tunes, the Big Band sound, and some country music. I try to keep those cowboys happy."Charles said with a quick "Yeeha."

Bill laughed. "Eric mentioned that you spent some time in the United States."

"Yes, three years. Performing all around your country. It was a pivotal event in my life. I learned so much music and a great deal about America's people and customs."

"I would be interested in learning what you liked and disliked."

"The Americans are an optimistic people. They have a can do mentality."

"Charles pours Bill and Eric a little Scotch and water that was brought to him when he sat down."

"For that reason I have explained to the band and our performers, that Americans like happy endings-as in their movies. It is difficult to find an American movie that does not have a challenge, with a happy ending.

Charles lifts each corner of his mouth to make a smile.

"The jitter bug and Swing are everywhere," Bill said.

Charles agreed, "Our music and songs will now have to reflect that reality."

Eric and Bill both nod their heads.

"You are right. We want to beat up the Bully, find the fortune, then ride into the sunset, with our gal riding by our side."

Charles, shaking his head, "I also learned that Americans enjoy their Fridays, and can create riots on Saturdays."

"You must have been in Chicago, or Oklahoma."

"No, it was what they call a Fandango. It was in Laredo, Texas. "Hot weather, hot food, and hot women. I think they were fighting over a gal named, Ida. She was a pretty gal. Looked like a princess from Fairyland.

"Cowboys, and *Indians*."

"Cowboys fighting mostly. But I did bring back a ten-gallon hat. He had received a knock- out blow, and never returned to pick it up."

When I was a kid, it was, "Finders – Keepers, losers - weepers."

"I liked the friendly openness of the people. A willingness to help others. Part of their pioneer spirit I would think."

"There was a time not that long ago, when the next family would live twenty miles away from you. Only by helping each other, could you survive." Charles said, as he looked to see who had entered, and if the crowd was getting restless.

"The music. Oh God-the music. It came out of every radio, and dance hall." Then with and with an American accent, "Every Honky-Tonk Café." Charles stopped for a moment, remembering those days, riding Lowrey's, when only the music mattered.

"The music filling the air. Bright and vibrant. Music that was alive in a way I had never felt before.

" Piano's in the Parlor. That was my earliest memories. Then phonographs and the radio."

"I remember. The hum of commerce, the science and industry; it was astonishing at times."

It still astounds me. I can remember the milk wagons coming to town, and doctors on horseback. The first streetlights turning night into day. A machine, that could fly through the air."

"And the things you did not like?" Bill asked, seeing a slight discomfort in Charles face.

"What I did not like? Poverty has always depressed me. Be it the slums of London, isolated coal towns, tobacco farms or street beggars in the cities." Charles paused a moment, knowing the racist policies in the English settlements.

The racism, and segregation I saw.

"It is America's original sin. With help from English and European slave ships."

Eric and Bill both nod their heads.

Everyone is equal when it comes to dying. Your military is enacting its own version of Jim Crow rules, here, in Britain. *I have heard on the streets*, "Boy get off the sidewalk. What are you doing talking to a white woman?"

Bill remained silent for a moment, having already heard about the race riot at Brandon bridge, in Preston. "A great Civil War was fought, to determine if all men are created equal. If we are a nation of, by and for the people. That battle is still being fought."

"I can only hope that final battle is won." Charles said, "Your Black soldiers have come to fight Germans, but must fight White Americans first. One Black soldier was thrown off a London Bus by White American soldiers."

Bill shook his head. "America is a work in progress. I can only hope that one day, it will live up to its promise."

"Till then, you hobble yourself. Your Black soldiers proved themselves, when fighting under French officers, in the first great war."

"As they did in the American civil War. A segregated military is something that I have spoken out, against."

"I would speak more forcefully. One Black soldier I met, told me the war got him out of the White man's kitchen, put a rifle in his hand, with orders to kill white folk, called Germans and Italians. He said he thought it was good training. For what he didn't say."

Charles pauses for a moment. "Yet, with Europe tearing itself apart, how can I complain about America? At least they are not killing themselves by the millions."

"War is incomparable in its horror and brutality. Quoting Sherman, an American General, "War. It's all Hell, and nothing butt.""

They all agreed. Bill then asked again about Charles travels. "Ever going back?"

"Maybe. Yet, I would not have traded the experience of traveling through America, for any other event in my life. I have seen the future that will occur after this war is over. With all the nations of Europe and Asia laid waste, that future will come from America. That I am sure of.

Eric nods his head as Bill smiles.

"Last man standing. We are protected by two vast oceans. Our cities have not been bombed, or our factories destroyed."

Eric sees that the band is motioning to Charles. Alice is peeking around the stage curtain.

"Charles, Alice is ready."

Charles looks up and sees Alice in her costume, waiting for him to introduce her.

"Gentlemen, I cannot keep a lady waiting."

Both Bill and Eric smile and nod their heads.

"Looks like our Nightingale is next."

"Great."

Charles runs up the side steps, and goes to the middle of the stage, grabbing the microphone. Charles takes on an American accent.

"OK. Quiet in the peanut Gallery, we got a lady here."

The crowd quiets down, a little surprised at the accent. Then in a loud and commanding voice. Charles yells out, "Now you Gents listen up. Alice is gonna sing a song.

"You all behave yourselves. Don't be sticking any gum under the table. And all you tobacco chewers, no spitting on the dance floor.

Don't need anyone slipping or sliding."

Charles walks in front of the band and lifts his baton. He will be "Alexander" leading his Rag Time Band. The music starts and Alice waits for her cue as the Americans recognize the song.

♪   "Oh ma honey, oh ma honey, Better hurry and
move along. Ain't you goin', ain't you goin'?
To the leader man, that ragged meter man?"

Alice gives a really beautiful, loving look, with her body sway-
ing, using her hands to beckon them to her.

♪   "Oh ma honey, oh ma honey, let me take you
by the hand, to Alexander's Rag Time Band."

Alice walks a little, turning her back slightly to the soldiers and
looking back over her shoulder.

♪   Ain't you comin' along?

Charles and some of the band members join in with Alice on
the Chorus.

♪   CHORUS:
Come on and hear, come on and hear, Alexan-
der's Ragtime Band. Come on and hear, come
on and hear, it's the best band in the land!
Jenny also sings as she takes drinks to a table.
They can play a bugle call like you never heard
before. A horn player stands up and plays.
"So natural that you wanna dance on the floor."

Alice pauses and smiles and looks out at the soldiers.

♪   "They're the best band in the land, honey
     lamb."

Alice gives a come-hither look and beckons the men with her
hand.

♪   Come on along, come on along, Let me take
     you by the hand.

Alice turns to Charles, using her thumb in a slight motion, as if
hitching a ride, pointing to Charles.

♪   "To meet the man who's the leader of the
     band! And if you care to hear the Swanee
     River, played in ragtime, then come on and
     hear, come on and hear, Alexander's Ragtime
     Band!

"The crowd cheers as Alice, Charles and all the band hold for a
moment, allowing the clapping and cheers to lessen.

♪   Oh ma honey, Oh ma honey, there's a fiddle
     with notes that screech.
     A Fiddle player from the band jumps up and
     plays a few bars of music.
     Like a preacher when he gives his speech. And
     the clarinet, is a sound you can't forget.

Charles plays a few notes.

♪ Ringing in your ears like a thunderclap.

The band members clap their hands.

♪ Come and listen, come and listen - better hurry along to listen to ALEXANDER'S RAG TIME BAND.

Alice leaves. Charles in a very proper and polite English accent. Alice, my dear, your adoring audience demands your return.

"Eric goes up to the stage with Bill. Eric to escort Alice back to the table, and Bill to speak with Charles.

"Charles, your mastery of American music and dialect, astounds me."

"Thank you. Three years traveling and playing music in your country; it provided me with many hours of practice and performances."

"And that American accent. I could have sworn you were from Texas, or some town in the Mid -West.

Charles, in a very English accent, in a funny, inward-looking moment, he turned to the crowd of Americans and then turning to Bill, "Three years in America, changes you."

"Looks like Jenny is meeting some of the Boys."

Jenny, going around taking drinks to tables and giving a big smile as she gets her tips.

"Jenny's been serving drinks lately. Once she found out how much the Americans tip."

"With those songs and that smile. I am not surprised."

"She gets all the chocolate she can eat." Charles said with a laugh.

Alice comes back to the table with Eric and joins Bill, Jenny and Charles.

"Alice, Good to see you. That was a wonderful performance.

"Thank you, General Morris."

"Please, Bill."

"I find it much more difficult to call a General, Bill, than I did a Colonel. But I shall try." Alice said as she smiled.

"Bill laughed, then asked, "You and Jenny do your own choreography?"

"Just Charles and I. Charles is old vaudeville, and Burlesque."

Alice reaches out and holds Charles hand, in a way a daughter would hold her father's hand.

Bill then told Charles, "You're a master of the Stage. You and Alice could perform on Broadway."

"I would love to perform in your country". Alice said, as Charles only smiled. "But after this war, I think that Eric and I will find a lovely home to raise a family."

"I can only wish the both of you, the best. Broadway just lost their brightest star." Bill suggested.

Jenny is serving drinks and as she turns away from the table, a man who seems drunk, pats her on the rear and Jenny jumps forward and gives a little shrink."

A man at the same table pulls him back into his chair, and then stands between the man who patted her and Jenny.

Bill starts to stand up and Alice motions Bill to sit.

"Jenny can take care of herself; she is a comedian. Give her a few moments."

Jenny turns to the man who is still standing and protecting her. "Thank you, Sir Galahad."

The man smiles. Jenny noticed that he was tall, dark, and handsome.

"You're welcome, my lady." Jenny smiles at him and then points her finger at the band, who have a song prepared for these events. The band starts up.

♪   Once on this Island' there dwelt, a dark eyed maiden.

Jenny pulls two fingers across her eyes, as if she is that dark eyed maiden.

♪   She lived all alone in a little log homed, where she reigned as a Queen.

Jenny takes on a regal look. Then pointing to the man who patted her on the rear.

♪   Till one day a stranger appeared on the scene.

Jenny looks at the man who patted her with great displeasure. Said he:

♪   Why waste your time, in this awful clime?

Jenny holds out her hand as if to see if it's raining and looks up to the skies for a moment, then pulls the collar of an imaginary coat together, then pretending to be the man who would take her away, Jenny made her voice deeper, and more masculine, starts to sing again,

♪ Oh come with me, my pretty Maiden, To my home across the sea.

Jenny then turns to all the crowd in the café and shouts out.

♪ But he went red, when she quickly said:

Jenny starts to dance in front of the man who patted her rear.

♪ I wouldn't leave my little wooden hut for you."
I've got one lover and I don't want two.

The crowd roars and the man who patted Jenny turns red.

♪ My beau is a man of arms.

Jenny points to Carlos.

♪ If he should come along, what might happen - there'll be no knowing.

Then looking at the man who patted her.

♪ So, you better be a going.
Before he looks for you.

The crowd laughs as Alice smiles in a knowing manner. Charles laughs, even though he has seen it before.

♪ "Just then a man of arms came in sight with a sword and a knife, ready to fight."

Jenny turns to the man who is standing and still protecting her and gets close to him and gently strokes his right arm from shoulder to elbow.

♪ Then said the maiden, stranger you'd better be a going, This man of arms, you see, is my beau'

Jenny again points at Sir Galahad,

♪ And he seems to want to strike a blow.

Jenny swings her arm at the man who patted her, as if she held a sword.

♪ Oh, is that true?' said the stranger as he looked for the door; running so fast his feet hardly touching the floor.

The song ends and the crowd roar their approval. The man who patted Jenny, sinks into his chair. Jenny gives a big smile and bows to the cheers.

"That's why I missed this place. Nothing like Alice and Jenny across the pond."

Eric, with an admiring look, "She's one of a kind."

"What was that song?" Bill asked.

"It's an old English song that, as Jenny says, she "Borrowed.""

"She can borrow to her hearts content." Bill offered.

Jenny walks through the crowd and smiles as she gets more applause and cheers.

Alice looks at Bill.

Jenny nears the table where Bill, Eric and Alice are seated.

"Well, you sent one soldier crawling under the table." Bill said.

Jenny smiles. "He'll behave himself now."

They all nod their heads.

CHAPTER 18

HOME OFFICE

The secretary looked up, "Hello Colonel. It's been a while. Please have a seat."

Eric sits down and looks around, noticing that things have not changed. Yet, people are more relaxed, not the air of doom in the room, as before.

"You may go in now."

"Colonel. Please come in." General Anderson said.

"Yes, Sir. Reporting as ordered, Sir."

"It has been a while since I last called you. I have followed your endeavors. Your commanders speak highly of you."

"Thank you, Sir."

"We have pushed out of the pocket and have advanced towards Caen. In a few months, we will march to the German border."

"It has been a day long in coming, Sir." Eric Said.

"Yes, it is the end game." General Anderson agreed.

"That is the belief of most officers. Colonel, you are being given another very sensitive assignment. The location of the V-1 rockets has been determined. The supreme allied command wants to stop the launches and obtain the rockets and technology. You have been chosen, on behalf of his majesties government, with General Morris to represent the government of the United States. Once again you will be working with General Morris.

Colonel, you are a staff officer within the Supreme Allied Command. Your knowledge of our plans, strategy, and resources, make you a walking code book, of our greatest secrets. You are to stay away from the battlefield. Also, make sure General Morris does also. The American ambassador has informed us that General Morris can become a "Wild Bill" Hickock."

"Yes, Sir. I understand." Eric responded, with a slight smile.

"These are your orders." General Anderson handed Eric his orders. There are new weapons that Germany is ready to release against London. A new kind of missile. Much more powerful than the buzz bomb we have had to deal with. You are to accompany Gen. Morris, who will be searching for these new weapons.

"Yes, Sir. I will work to the best of my abilities."

"His majesty's government wants this innovative technology, as much as the Americans and Russians do."

"I understand."

"You are dismissed, Colonel. Good Luck."

"Yes, Sir."

Eric leaves General Anderson's office.

CHAPTER 19

ALICE'S FLAT

"Alice enters her apartment, allowing Eric to come in as she pulls the keys from the door. Alice closes the door as Eric hangs his coat and helps Alice with her coat. Eric then turned to Alice, holds her, pulling her towards him.

Eric opening his arms, "When we are married, this will be the best part of the day. Coming home to you, my love." Eric gives Alice a long kiss.

"The moment that I long for each day." Alice simple said, taking a step forward, going on her toes, to have him hold her and lift her, as he once did, but not daring to transfer her weight to him, uncertain of his strength, his injury. Alice then pulled back, feeling Eric losing his balance. "I have promised you dinner. Just the two of us. I would keep my man well feed, and well attended to."

Eric pulls Alice towards him for another kiss, then Alice smiles and leaves his arms.

"We will share a romantic dinner. With candles and soft music. A night in the arms of the man, I love."

"I shall do all in my power to make your wishes come true."

"Alice gives a smile of love and desire but pushes Eric away so that she can start dinner."

"I have prepared dinner, I have only to place it in the oven. You may help me set the table."

Eric gives a slight nod of the head, as Alice walks to the ice box, and takes out a pan and places it into the oven.

"The tablecloth and candles are in the upper drawer. Alice said as she pointed to its location.

Eric finds the tablecloth in the kitchen drawer. He started to spread the tablecloth over the table. Alice comes over to help him. Alice turned and picked up the candles, and places one candle on the table as Eric lights that candle. Alice grabs the other candle and uses the lit one to light her candle.

Do you still remember our vows for our wedding day?" Alice started, as Eric waited for his turn. "We are two candles that now share one light. A light of love that will help us through our trials, and tears."

Eric then said his part. " My this light heal this poor world that now knows only darkness and grief. So that our children can be safe and joyful."

Eric reaches over and grabs both of Alice's hands in his. Then they each grabbed their candles and bot lighted one candle, together. Repeating there prepared marriage vows.

"We are two candles that now share one light, and one life. All that I am, all that I shall become, belongs to you. You full fill me." Alice gives a loving look at Eric and squeezes his hands.

"All my wishes and all my desires rest in your heart and hands." Eric reached out to Alice. .

"Eric moves around the table and embraces Alice again. Then Eric looks up as he sniffs the air.

"We're having lamb, aren't we?"

Alice jumps back from Eric and turns to the stove, as she moves towards it.

"I've already partially cooked the lamb. It needed only a little while. I would not spoil such a beautiful evening by burning dinner."

"Thank you."

"Alice puts on a romantic record and then sits down with Eric for dinner. The candle lights flicker and dinner is over and the table cleaned. Alice is sitting next to Eric with her head on his shoulder.

"Alice, I need to tell you something. I will be gone for a time."

Alice sits up, looking a little shocked and worried at the same time.

"You're not being sent to the front?"

"No. It seems that I know too much and have become too valuable to risk."

"Alice relaxes a moment."

"When will you be back. We are so close to ending this war. Why are they sending you now?"

Alice pauses, knowing she should not have asked such a question.

"Yes, close-but not over. That is really all I can tell you."

"Alice relaxes for a moment."

"At least you will not be at the front."

"Far from it. I will be with command headquarters."

Alice gives a slight smile.

"During the retreat to Dunkirk, knowing you were fighting; not knowing if you were alive or dead. Each night I prayed that you would come back to me. Then hearing that you were hurt, injured. Not being allowed to visit you."

Alice falls back into Eric's open arms and looks up at Eric as her head rests on his chest."

"Not knowing if I could live without you."

"We are destined to be together - forever. I feel this with all my being. We are one, heart and soul." Eric said.

"We share one heartbeat."

Alice reaches over and pulls the chain on the living room lamp and the room darkens.

CHAPTER 20

COTTON-EYED JOE

It is the fourth of July, 1944. The allied landing has been successful. The English and Canadian armies are on the verge of taking Caen, American troops have liberated Cherbourg and are surrounding Saint Lo.

Russian troops have liberated the Crimea and Ukraine and now are moving into Poland. Victory is in the air, but London is now under attack by the V1 and V2 rockets.

Charles Addressed the crowd. "Ladies and Gentlemen, we have a special performance tonight for our American friends. For this day, is the fourth of July." Cheers from the American soldiers were heard. We will not go into the details as to why this is a special day for the Americans.

"Yet, let us celebrate together. I have listened to requests for country music by the men from Kentucky, Tennessee and Texas, and those states in between.

"I have played country music at fairs, ho-downs, and once, at the Grand Old Opry.

Cheers from parts of the crowd.

"So, relax. The final act will begin in the next few minutes."

Eric and Bill are sitting at their favorite table. Bill smiles and waves at Alice and Jenny who both wave back.

"This should be fun. Charles is going to make a lot of men happy. Gives them a little bit of home."

"Charles amazes me with his versatility. I have never really heard country music."

"Country music comes from the heart. You will hear America talking to you, in this music."

Eric starts to enjoy the night and a some drinks. "*It is my first full day off in weeks. A night to relax is, sorely needed.*"

"You got that right. I am taking Charles advice. Relax and have a drink."

This war is ending. We finally can relax.

"Cherbourg has been liberated. We have surrounded Saint Lo."

Bill slaps the table with a look of triumph.

"With mastery of the air, this war is entering its final stages. One pilot I talked to, told me he was flying low, following the road back to Germany, and can across twenty German troop transports The transports were all in a straight line. . His guns had not been used that day. He opened up. Curious how many he had killed, he circled around. He said there were over forty dead, laying on the ground. A number of transports burning.

"So close to home. Now, so far away." Bill said, with no emotion on his face.

"Now, if only we can find the buzz bomb launch sites." Eric said, as he pointed to the sky.

Bill nodded his head as Charles gets the band ready.

"Bill, I would like to request a favor from you."

"You got it." Bill said, "I will be spending six weeks on a special assignment. With these buzz bombs starting to strike London, and Alice working late, I wonder if you might assist her at times . She refuses to go to the shelters."

"I can assist in such ways that Alice allows me. Alice is a head strong woman. She got's more spunk and courage than you might think. Yes, of course. It would be a pleasure."

Both Bill and Eric, knowing they will finish the conversation later, start to watch Charles.

"Take your seats. Ladies and Gentlemen, the final act is about to begin."

The band strikes up the first few bars of Cotton Eyed Joe, as the Americans and Canadians cheer, immediately recognizing the song.

"Feel free to join in." Charles said.

Alice smiles at Eric and looks to an engagement ring on her finger. She holds it, to show Jenny.

"Charles has another song that has just enthralled me. It must be quintessential Americana." Alice announced.

"I liked it too." Jenny said. " Charles says it's his favorite country music song."

"Well then, let me get ready." Bill grabs his drink and finishes it off. Eric smiles, grabs his drink, and also finishes it. Charles walks to the microphone again.

In a very English accent, "Now for a song all North America knows. They danced to it in Calgary Canada, and Austin Texas. Then in a very American accent, Now listen up all you country folk. I wanna see clapping, foot stomping, and dancing to, "Cotton Eyed Joe".

The music starts. Cheers go up from the crowd and a Canadian soldier jumps to his feet and starts to dance at his table. A Canadian woman in uniform, walks by and grabs his hand, as they both walk to the stage.

Charles sings the song is a very heavy country music style.

Cotton eyed Joe, Cotton eyed Joe, where did you come from, where did you go? Where did you come from Cotton eyed Joe?

The Canadian soldiers start to dance, doing a lot of fast foot moves and dancing in a wild manner.

"If it hadn't been for Cotton eyed Joe, I'd been married forty years ago. Where did you come from, where did you go, where did you come from Cotton eyed Joe?"

"My gal was pretty as she could be.

She wanted to - marry me."

Charles grabs the mic and leans it over, like he is kissing a woman.

"If it hadn't been for Cotton eyed Joe I'd been married forty years ago. Where did you come from, where did you go, where did you come from?

Cotton eyed Joe?"

Charles has the band play just the music in a fast tempo.

The Canadian soldiers do some more fancy foot work and struts. Thumb in arm pit, fingers straight up.

♪   "If it hadn't been for Cotton eyed Joe I'd been married a long time ago. Where did you come from, where did you go? Where did you come from Cotton eyed Joe?"

The Canadian soldier mentions his elbows, twirls and gets ready to end with a few more quick steps.

♪   "Cotton eyed Joe, Cotton eyed Joe, what did I do to make you treat me so. If it hadn't been for Cotton eyed Joe, I'd been married forty years ago. Where did you come from, where did you go, where did you come from

Cotton eyed Joe?"

The music ends and the crowd cheers, as the Canadian soldiers take a bow. Charles motions to the band to take a bow and then Charles takes a bow. An American soldier takes the floor, addressing the Canadian soldiers.

Frank offered, "Aw, who taught you Canadians how to dance Cotton Eyed Joe. That might be some fancy pants dancing, but that is not how you dance Cotton eyed Joe. Come on Tennessee.

"Right behind ya-Kentuc." Two American nurses follow onto the floor.

"You're not leaving Texas out of this one.

All eight Americans stand next to each other, getting ready to do a line dance.

"Sir, the extended version, please." Frank requested.

"You got it!" Charles shouted out in return.

Charles throws his head back and gets ready for a rocking, soulful version of Cotton Eyed Joe. The band starts up again and the line dance starts.

♪ If it hadn't been for Cotton eyed Joe I'd been married forty years ago. Where did you come from, where did you go, where did you come from Cotton eyed Joe.

Cotton eyed Joe, Cotton eyed Joe - what did I do to make you treat me so. You took my gal (in a whining, complaining voice) away from me. Took her plum to Tennessee,

High steps in the line dance.

♪ "If it hadn't been for Cotton eyed Joe I'd been married forty years ago. Where did you come from, where did you go, where did you come from Cotton eyed Joe.

More line dancing with a shuffle and a two step move.

♪ " Cotton eyed Joe, Cotton eyed Joe, his eyes were crossed, and he was mean, but he was tall, and he was lean, and my gal, she just kept, following him.

Line dance continues with some more country foot steps.

♪ If it hadn't re did you go, where did you come from, Cotton eyed Joe.

Charles gives a look and a shake of the head.

♪ My gal was as pretty as she could be. She had beautiful hair and eyes as bright as I'd ever seen. Lips so red, white dresses so clean, she was just the prettiest thing.

Charles shows some pain and loss in the next few verses.

♪ If it hadn't been for Cotton eyed Joe I'd been married forty years ago. Where did you come from, where did you go, where did you come from Cotton eyed Joe?

More line dancing.

♪ I loved that gal with all my heart, and she promised we'd never part. But then she ran away with that Cottoned eyed Joe! What did I do to make her treat me so ?

More line dancing.

♪ Cotton eyed Joe, Cotton eyed Joe, I would have married that gal of mine, we had already set the time.

Charles looks down for a moment, then looks up and with a voice in pain, partly sings and partly saying the words.

♪   If it hadn't been for Cotton eyed Joe I'd been married a long time ago. Where did you come from, where did you go? Where did you come from Cotton eyed Joe?

Charles gets a standing ovation and cheers. Charles takes a few more bows as the crowd gives a standing ovation.

Bill turned to Eric. "I'm starting to wonder if Charles is really American, pretending to be English."

"Charles is full of surprises."

Charles walks over and smiled as the soldiers on nearby clap as he walks by.

"Charles, I could arrange a tour of America?"

"Thank you. But I have done that. I am back home now - in England. I serve in the home guard. Another Englishman who has returned. In my own way, I serve king and country."

"Well said!"

Alice greeted Charles, "Just wonderful Charles. I knew that song would bring the house down."

"Jenny stands up and locks her arm around Charles arm."

"We're going to be doing duets together. I want to make sure he does not replace me with his own act." Jenny remarked.

"Love, I will keep you till you grow old and gray."

"Don't say those things." Jenny said.

"Or until a handsome American takes you away."

Jenny smiled shyly.

"I see who meets you at the stage door." Charles remarked'

"And from Los Angeles. Right next to - Hollywood." Alice added.

Bill and Eric laugh as Charles and Alice smile.

"Tall, dark, and handsome still works. I have been promised all the fish and chips, and Chocolate I could ever eat. I give half to the children now."

With a sickly look, Alice said, "You can have my chocolate. I can not eat any more."

CHAPTER 21

———

HOME OFFICE

Gen. Anderson is talking to Eric. "Colonel, I have orders from the PM."

He hands Eric the documents.

"I have requested that General Morris be present, since the both of you are well acquainted and have similar assignments. As we all know, even the best of friends, have arguments. Both our militaries want to find the site, where these new missiles are located."

"Making sure that we stay united as allies, not racing each other, to obtain this recent technology, is the demand of the PM and the Supreme Allied Commander."

General Morris walks in and is greeted by Eric and General Anderson.

"Ike has given me orders to have discussions with English officers, and Field Commanders in Europe, informing them of what we seek. I will be back in London, in three weeks.

"I'm sure both of you want to discuss the matter and make certain that the message is the same. The technology will be shared."

"I believe that most staff officers perceive the danger that infighting, and glory hounds can cause. I have been told to accompany field headquarters, as we push forward, into those places we believe the launch sites are located. I am not sure when I well be back."

"I am confident that you both will be able to get the message out, to the officers and men, and find these missiles, before London is attacked again. Please use my office."

Gen. Anderson leaves.

"I had hoped I could get back into this war, but Eisenhower knows me to well. He's already made sure, that under no circumstances am I to be given a battlefield command. The search for the launch site is about as close as I will get."

"I have not fared any better."

"Your much to valuable. I also follow orders."

"As we all must do," Eric responded Ed.

"I still think that I might have a chance to get back into action. I am still trying to pull some strings back in Washington." Bill said Eric turns to Bill and in a sad voice admits the truth.

"I am afraid there are no strings above Churchill, that I can pull."

"I expect to finish my assignment after I visit Field command. Dispatches have already been sent as to what we seek. Although, I will not depart for two weeks. I need to assist in the final review of operational plans for the occupation of Germany."

CHAPTER 22

ROCKETS

Go easy on meat and butter. Two ounces is of butter is allowed per week The door to Alice's flat is opened and Alice enters her flat with Bill behind her.

"Please come in, Bill." Alice said as she pulled the light cord.

"Thank you."

Alice smiles at Bill. "As, I promised, let me make you some tea."

"Having tea in an English home is always a treat."

Alice offered a true friendship. " I will extend an open invitation for you to join Eric and I, whenever you are in England."

"I appreciate that."

"Eric informed me that you would be coming to The Torch Café, to assist me. Thank you." Alice's look lingered on Bill's face. As Alice came over to Bill, and passed him the cup, "Thank You."

"It's my pleasure. It would be hard to keep me away from The Torch Café. It's the best show this side of the Atlantic."

"Compliments are appreciated. Alice pauses, setting out the scones.

Alice then asked, "Hopefully, your fellow Americans, at the Embassy, have adapted to life in England?"

" They seem to be enjoying themselves. Although I have cautioned a few of the embassy guard, that a pub was not a bar or Saloon. More like a club for the neighbor. Wives, Mothers, and grandmother go there.

"You are right. Still, I wish to express my thanks. At times, the taxi's are hard to get late at night."

"Sure, glad to help. Any word from Eric?" Bill asked.

"He expects to be back in a month." Alice said.

"Good. There is nothing more uncertain than war, and where one will be stationed."

"For how long? It seemed forever when Eric was fighting in France. "You'll manage - you got spunk and spirit." Bill proclaimed, as Alice gave a lite laugh, and smiled. Bill decides to change the subject and starts to look out the window of Alice's flat. "You have a very nice view of London."

"Sometimes I'll pull my chair against the window and just relax. Watch the lights go out, as London starts to slumber." Hoping the sirens, the searchlights do not fill the sky.

Bill sees a rocket flame crossing the night sky. Then striking the ground about 300 yards away. Bill immediately knowing that the sound boom will bust out the windows.

Bill screams out. "Alice!"

Alice is walking to the table, when she hears Bill and stops. Bill tackles Alice and takes her to the corner of the kitchen, covering her with his body. The sound boom hits and the glass from the window shatters and covers the room."

"My God."

Bill lets go of Alice. Bill seems a little shaken also.

"It was a rocket."

"What?" Alice asked, having never heard the term.

"A rocket. Something that we hoped the Germans only had a few of." Pausing for reflection, Bill then informed Alice, "Three days ago, there was a large explosion in London. So, as not to panic the public, you did not get the truth about that explosion."

"I read about a gas explosion." Alice exclaimed, then looking out the broken window, seeing the black smoke, hearing the sirens of the fire Trucks.

Bill simply said, "You were told that there was an explosion in a gas pipe. Well, unless there are gas pipes that fly, that was a rocket."

"A rocket?"

"That was no buzz bomb. The Germans call it their victory rocket, or V1."

"Can it be stopped?"

"Bill pauses for a moment, then slowly shakes his head no.

"No. You're going to find out in a few days any way. It's a new type of weapon. It travels near the edge of space; at a speed we estimate at 3000 miles an hour. We have no defenses against it.

"Then once again, London is under attack!"

"Yes."

Alice regains her composer, straightening out her dress and looks at Bill. Then in a calm, firm voice, speaks out. "We will endure, as we always have."

Bill smiles at Alice, admiring her spirit. "Alice, I sometimes wonder if Eric realizes what a lucky man he is. What a package."

"I always seem to be thanking you. Thank you. Being at my wedding with a face cut from flying glass, would not have been something I would have looked forward to."

Bill smiles and gives a little bow of the head.

"I am now assuming that I will be given an invitation to the wedding."

"I can assure you; it will be the first invitation that I send."

"Another V1 rocket hits, but much further away. Alice stiffens for a moment as Bill sees the flash in the distance. Alice grabs a broom and pushes glass off the seats and then away from the table."

"I have promised you tea, and rockets will not stop me."

Bill laughs and looks at Alice with admiration.

"Nothing's going to stop you, Alice. Now, for good conversation and a cup of tea. You keep your promises.

"You shall have your cup of tea."

Alice closes the curtains, as the blackout sirens sound and give warning again. Alice sits and quietly talks to Bill. . After a time , Bill sees that Alice is getting tired. .

"Thank you. It has been an eventful night - with tea, scones, and pleasant company."

Bill gets up from the table and helps Alice with her chair. Alice moves towards the door and unlocks it, to allow Bill to leave. Alice stops at the door frame as Bill turns to say goodbye.

"Once again, thank you."

Alice kisses Bill on the cheek as a thank you. Bill smiles a smile that says, "Thank You lovely lady."

The landlady is looking around the corner and sees Alice kiss Bill.

"A gentle reward from a gentle, and gentile Lady. Thanks."

Bill leaves Alice.

The landlady hurries back into her flat as Bill sees her, then passes by.

Another officer, Jim, soon comes by to check on Alice and meets the Landlady.

Jim called out to the landlady, as he entered the hallway. "I saw the broken glass in the window. I stopped to make sure that Alice had not been hurt."

"She's fine. She had company most the night." The Landlady said, as she smiled and waited to see if Jim is interested in her gossip, then continued.

"She gave that American General a big kiss, at three in the morning. He must take her home each night."

"They spend lots of time together?" Jim asked.

"At night they seem to. She's made her bed." The landlady said, Jim looks a little surprised but continues to listen.

"To think her fiancée is over in Europe-fighting. He's been cuckolded."

Jim looks at her and then turns away and moves to leave the building.

CHAPTER 23

LIES

Eric has returned from France, now having heard that Jim is spreading lies about Alice, his is on a hunt and destroy mission. He has come to the officer's rest area, after hearing that Jim is there. Jim and two officers are standing, having a conversation.

Eric walks quickly up to Jim. "I have heard of your lies about Alice, I will not remain silent.

"Eric swings and knocks Jim to the ground. The two other officers grab hold of Eric and hold him back."

Eric shouted at Jim."I have fought many men in my life, and I am more than capable of dealing with a lie from a scoundrel . Get up."

Eric is ready to knock Jim down again.

"That American General was with Alice all night." Jim shouted back.

"I requested that he escort her home. He stayed with her during a rocket attack!"

Jim and the two other officers are stunned at the fury of Eric's attack on Jim. One officer calls out.

"Attention."

General Anderson comes in with General Morris beside him. Bill has also heard of the rumors and is very mad.

"Captain. I have been told by General Morris that you have cast a shadow on his honor as a gentleman and an officer. The friction you are causing will not be tolerated."

"If you were in my army, I would deal with you the same way that Eric just dealt with you."

"Eric, I understand your anger. Yet, you should have reported the incident to my office."

Eric responds with great anger in his voice.

"Yes Sir."

"Captain you must apologize to General Morris immediately. And to Eric."

"General Morris I wish to extend my apologies. I am sorry if my words caused offense."

"Your apology is not accepted." General Morris turns and storms out the room. Now General Anderson is mad, and he knows that if he cannot restore good relations with the American officer corps, he will be the one in trouble.

General Anderson addressed the officers in the area. Gen, Anderson turns to the other officers in the room. "Any officer spreading vile rumors about fellow officers, or our allies, will face stern disciplinary measures."

General Anderson looked a various officer, with his gaze settling on Jim. "Gentleman, we have taken a heavy toll in the Officers corps, as we push towards Germany. More officers are needed for a new offensive, Market Garden. I will first ask for volunteers.

Addressing Jim, "Captain, you are being sent to join our forces as we move further towards Germany. I shall first ask for volunteers, before I notify a few more officers of their new orders." Then looking directly at Jim. "Captain, you have a skill set in communications that is needed at the front. You will be sent with the officers to be sent.

Jim looks speechless for a moment. "Yes, Sir. Sir, is this a punishment?"

"When does fighting for kith and kin, king and country, become a punishment? Be ready tomorrow. I would think winning distinction on the battlefield would be something you would relish. I receive letters daily from officers requesting to be sent to a fighting unit. To win a battlefield promotion.

You have your orders and will obey. Headquarters have instructed all commanding officers to remove from military service, those with a defeatist mentality, or shrinks from their duties, are to be removed from military service. Those so charged will face charges of cowardice in the face of the enemy."

General Anderson, and Eric walked to General Anderson's office, where Bill was waiting. "I think the two of you might want to talk."

"I went and talked to Alice after I heard of the rumors. She needed to know about the wagging tongue, the lies of her Landlady. She will be moving."

"That Landlady, is a witch. With a fealty mind."

"I will be helping Alice move to another flat.

"Good." Bill loudly remarked.

Eric then said, "Alice told me of the rocket attack and how you saved her from injury. Thank you."

"I hope you did not question Alice about those rumors."

There is a long silence, as Eric looks embarrassed.

"I had hoped for a resounding - NO! Eric, I cannot believe that you did not trust a woman who loves you so deeply."

"Nor can I, now. I did not question her. I seed of doubt crossed my mind the day I heard. It is well known that Ike's driver, as did other women, for various reasons, provided additional benefits to Americans. One might say, "Above and beyond the call of duty."

"It was tea, scones, and pleasant conversation. And a kiss on the cheek for pushing her away from the blast. I thought it an ample reward from a gracious Lady."

"General Morris, I would not want this incident to end what I consider to be a friendship that I value."

Bill smiles and offers his hand to Eric. Eric quickly grabs his hand, and they shook. "I feel the same. It's going to take more than the lies of a fool, to end this friendship."

Eric looked relived. Glad to still be Bill's friend.

"Then mates."

"Yes, always have been."

CHAPTER 24

CHEWING GUM

Eric, Bill and Alice are in The Torch Café. Charles and Jenny are on the stage. Alice, Bill and Eric are sitting at the table.

"It's nice to have a few days to relax." Eric said said.

"You got that right." Bill said.

"With this war finally coming to an end, I have found myself with more leave. It's a nice experience." Eric said, agreeing with Bill, and seeing the joy on Alice's face. Eric then stated, "I cannot see this war lasting more than a few months. The Russians have crossed the Ord River and are moving quickly towards Berlin."

"A normal life once again. What a pleasure that will be. Although the practice of Law, has its own excitement."

"What do you expect to do first?" Alice asked. Looking intently at Bill.

"Go back to that farm, next to town, that I grew up on. Just relax. The only time I want to hear the word General, is when someone's talking about going to the general store in town.

"I have a similar idea." Eric said as he looked at the stage. "Looks like Jenny is getting ready for another song." Turning to Alice.

"What's the song?" Eric asked Alice.

This one's a surprise for Charles."

"What's it about?" Bill asked.

"Chewing gum."

"How can you write a song about chewing gum ?"

"You'll see. It's funny."

"I am surprised Jenny did not write a song about fish and chips."

Eric and Bill smile as Jenny goes up to the microphone.

"This is a new song I wrote. Something the band and I have put together for Charles's birthday."

Charles looks surprised, not knowing what Jenny has in store for him. The band members smile and start to play.

> ♪ Oh, how Charles hates chewing gum - every morning.

The band joins as Charles smiles.

> ♪ Every morning.
> It's on the glasses and in the sink. Under the tables - and under the seats. Oh, how Charles hates chewing gum every morning.

The band members echo Jenny.

> ♪ Every morning.
> Its on the doors and on the floors and even on

Jenny points at a dart board.

> ♪ The dart board, Oh, how Charles hates chewing gum every morning.

The band chimes in again.

♪ On the doors and on the floors and even on
the dart boards, every morning.

Charles gives a sad look and nods his head. Charles decides to join in on the next chorus.

♪ When their drunk,

Jenny points to her hair, then to a drunk, with his head on the table, it's in their hair. Then Jenny and the band all screamed at the same time,

♪ It's everywhere.

Charles joins in as a few Americans sitting at a table also decide to join in.

♪ Oh, how Charles hates chewing gum - every
morning.

The audience laughs as Charles nods his head, then joins in on the chorus.

♪ When they finish, they

Jenny uses her hands to pretend she is rolling up some gum.

♪ make it all round - And when it hits you,

Jenny pretends she is throwing chewing gum.

♪   it doesn't make a sound.

Charles acts as if he is very sad.

♪   Oh, how Charles hates chewing gum - every morning.

The audience laughed, then started to roar their approval. Jenny beams at the shouts and clapping. Charles tells the band to stand up, as Charles and the band welcome the applause from the audience, Charles, and the band take their hands and place them over their hearts, then throwing the hand out to the crowd. Charles's way of offering his heart felt thanks.

"I didn't think anyone could write a song about chewing gum. I stand corrected. Never again shall I doubt Jenny." Bill announced with admiration.

"Thank you for coming to our show. Ladies and Gentlemen, our license requires that we close at eleven. It is now ten past. To ensure that you can continue to come to, The Torch Café, to enjoy our show, please move towards the exits."

The crowd continues to talk and drink. They pay no attention to the "band man on the stand. Some men walk over to a dart board and begin to play. Turning to Jenny, who is now beside Charles.

"Oh dear. I better talk to the audience, before the bobbies show up, and arrange for my early retirement. I know one way to get them on their feet. Jenny, I will need you for a moment longer.

As Charles and Jenny walk down stage, to the edge, Frank, an American soldier calls out for another song.

"Aw come on. Just one more song!"

Charles goes to the mic on the stage and announces one more song.

CHAPTER 25

CRICKETS AND WICKETS

"Boys, I got one more song for ya. It's the seventh inning stretch. As done in England."

"Get up from those chairs and stretch those arms and legs."

The band starts up, with Charles and Jenny get close to the mic. The band starts, with Charles starting the song.

> ♪ Katie Jacquez, was Cricket crazy
>
> She had the longing the calling.
>
> And had it bad.
>
> One day she went to shout and scream. To create a scene, for the city team.
>
> Katie Jacquez was Cricket crazy, she has the disease and had it bad. Just to shout and scream for the city team, was her only day, and nighttime dream.
>
> Now, this was the only song she wished to sing.

A few band members get up with a cricket bat. Charles grabbed the mic in one hand and a ball in the other.

♪   On a Saturday, her young American soldier,
     came calling, asking for a date.
     Asking if Katie wanted to see a play, a movie,
     or dance the night away.
     Katie said no. Katie wanted to see her city
     team!
     So, Katie said, "This is where we will go."

The band stands up, as do all the Americans, and those others who want to participate. Alice also joins in with Jenny, knowing the song, and standing at the table.

Jenny starts the chorus, with Alice being quick to joined by Bill.

♪   Take me to the ball game
     I want to be London loud, with the crowd
     just buy me some chips, and give me a sip
     of your glorious beer.
     I don't care if I never go home.

Some Americans start to sing.

♪   For it's one, two, three stumps,
     you're out, at the old ball game.
     Katie Jacquez saw all the teams play, and knew
     the eleven players, by their salty names.

One band member pretends to make a pitch and another to swing the bat. Charles continues the song.

♪   When the score was five to five,
Katie Jacquez knew what to do.
She shouted loud and clear.
So that even West Minister could hear
For its wickets in cricket
Bowlers, pitches, bails on stumps
Not rumps.
Ten batters in white kits
Wanting to hit, at the old ball game.

Charles shouts, "Boys, join in, you know3 it now.

♪   Just buy me some chips, and give me a sip;
For it's one, two , three wickets,
you're out, at the old ball game.

The Café explodes. Men cheer Charles and Jenny again. It's one of those songs that take Americans back to their hometowns. Playing in the sandlots, and in front of their homes, with their fathers and brothers.

"Ladies and Gentlemen, my American friends, thank you for your kind applause. I truly appreciate you being here! Charles has a quiet moment as his statement has a double meaning. Charles knows that many will die in the coming months, the war with Japan not over. "Yet, I must obey the law, and now that I have all of you on your feet," many Americans start to laugh, the lights flickering out, "I must ask that we say adieu, adios, and a sincere good night."

All the men and women start to laugh again and in good spirits, head towards the door. Charles and Jenny head back to the table where Eric, Bill and Alice are sitting... "Charles, you made a lot of American soldiers happy. On behalf of the United States Army, Thank you." Turning to Jenny, "Jenny, you might be the next pin-up girl. Betty Grable better watch out."

CHAPTER 26

UNEXPECTED DEATH

Eric walks into General Anderson's office, and salutes.

General Anderson stood and returned the salute, then extended his hand. "Hello Colonel, I'm afraid I have some bad news for you."

"Yes Sir. I think a bit of bad news is something that we have all come to expect over these last six years.

"I wanted to be the one to tell you."

Eric stiffens up a bit.

"General Morris has been killed."

Eric stands stunned at the news. "I saw him three days ago, Sir. He was in London. We both where at the Torch Café, just three days ago!" Eric's voice trails off, seeing the certainty on General Anderson's face.

"He was in London, till two days ago." General Anderson stops for a moment.

"The American's found where the rocket scientists where hiding. An intelligence officer was needed to question them. General Morris volunteered.

Eric stands stiff, still not knowing what to say.

"In his possessions, there was a box, a gift to you and Alice. Letters to some friends. I think you might know who those friends are."

"Yes, Sir." Eric said, as he took hold of the letters, seeing them addressed to Alice, Jenny, Charles, and himself. Eric is still stunned and speechless, allowing his hands to drop to his side, with one letter falling to the ground, that he immediately picked up.

"The news has not been announced. I expect it will after a time. I do not think the Americans are in a hurry to announce the death of a General."

"I appreciate you telling me, Sir. It's stunning news. I would like to tell some of his other close friends."

"Yes, of course. You may tell them of his death. But not why or where he was killed. Request their silence, till the Americans make the announcement.

"Yes, Sir. I understand."

"It was an artillery barrage. General Morris was leading the scientists to transports."

General Anderson pulled out a box from behind his desk.

"He asked that a box kept in his office be given to you.

General Anderson handed the box to Eric.

"There's a card with it."

"My fiancée promised General Morris the first invitation for our wedding. Thank you, Sir. This will mean a lot to Alice, and I.

"The horror of war is that the best and the bravest, die."

"Yes Sir." Eric answered.

"I think it was an American General who said that "War is all hell and nothing but".

" Yes Sir. That was General Sherman, of the American Civil War, as General Morris informed me. I can only hope this poor, brutalized world remembers that.

"As we all do." General Anderson said, giving the same sentiment.

CHAPTER 27

FAREWELL TO THE TORCH CAFÉ

It is the 30th of January 1965. The state funeral of Winston Churchill is about to begin. Tens of thousands have waited all night, and into a bitter cold morning, to pay their respects. It has been twenty years since the war ended.

Charles unlocks the door and enters, The Torch Café. Charles is walking with a cane and appears much older now. Eric and Alice come in behind him.

"Not up to its former glory, but I can still rent the hall and subsidize my pension. It's all rock and roll." Charles said with some displeasure.

"When we traveled in Europe, that's all we seemed to hear."

"I do not receive much when I share the ticket sales with the rock bands.

"Those kids don't have much money to spend." Eric said.

"Although there were four lads from Liverpool, a few years ago. When they played, I filled the house. But they no longer perform here.

Alice asked, "Did they play a song called "Love Me Do?"

"Yes, and when I split the purse with them, I thought they "loved me too."

Charles smiles, as Alice and Eric laugh.

Alice then asked, "Charles, you don't listen to rock and roll on the radio?"

"Of course not!"

"Those lads from Liverpool have become very successful."

"I am not surprised. They started wearing suits on their last performance here. Although they still needed a haircut. Rock and roll is just a passing fad. I give it a few more years and wager it will be gone."

"I should hope so." Eric said.

The door opens and Jenny and Carlos come in.

Two teenage boys have come in with Jenny and her husband. They are Jenny's children.

Jenny runs for Alice, taking her coat off as she runs. With tears in her eyes, Alice runs to meet Jenny. They give a big hug and almost don't want to let go.

"Jenny, Jenny, so good to see you." Alice said, still holding to Jenny.

"It's been too long. The years just seemed to fly away; raising a family, getting used to a new country. Jenny said.

"How is life in California?"

"Different and exciting. Just as Charles said. It changes you."

Charles smiles and laughs. "I never lied to my Ladies."

"And these two fine lads. This must be your oldest. Hello Scott."

"Hello, nice to meet you." Scott answered.

"It is my pleasure to meet you."

Eric then said, "And mine also."

Charles spoke up, "Welcome to The Torch Café, young Master Scott.

Eric, Alice, and Charles look at Jenny and Scott and know that a deep wound that Jenny has carried, is healed.

"This is your youngest - John."

"John is fourteen. He answers to John or Juan. It helps if you live in LA."

How do you like living in Los Angeles?

"It's like living in the United Nations. From all over the world, they come to America.

Jenny, with excitement in her voice. "There are two English pubs within ten miles of my house. I can have fish and chips whenever I want. And in Venice Beach, I can order fish and chips in the middle of November!

"Fish and chips on the beach in November? I will have to visit you soon." Alice said, as she saw Jenny lean towards her man.

Charles sees that the crowds lining the streets, the funeral carriage has arrived at the cathedral, on the television. The funeral service about to begin. "I think they are getting ready for the services."

All become quite to pay their respects to Churchill.

Ladies and Gentlemen, we are gathered here to pay our respects to a great and heroic Englishman, Winston Spencer Churchill. Who led this nation through very dark and dangerous days. Let us first have a moment of silence.

All grow silent for a few moments. Eric bows his head, and the others follow.

"A toast, to Churchill. The indispensable man."

The glasses are raised for the toast, and everyone finishes their drink.

More toasts are offered.

To the Russians, Poles, Canadians, and Australians, who joined with us in that terrible struggle.

To our French allies, who fought so bravely and sacrificed so much.

The television announces a special song, requested by Churchill for his funeral.

"In a few moments, we will have some music, that Churchill requested in his will, to be played at his funeral. The Battle Hymen of the Republic." All listen for a few moments.

Eric lifts his glass. "To President Franklin Roosevelt."

Alice continues, "To those talkative, restless, people, the Americans." Alice stops for a time, thinking of the Americans she met at the Torch Café and of Bill.

"Eric continued the toasts, "To General William Morris, my friend Bill. A Thoughtful pause grabs hold of all. "To our friend Bill. Cheers everyone." Jenny said.

A loud cheer goes up from all. For a few moments as the light dims, all is silent.

Young Master Scott then spoke to Eric, my mother said you met Churchill?"

"Yes, I knew the Prime Minister." In a loud, firm, and proud voice. "I was there - when the lion roared."

All remain silent again as they see that the services are ending.

"I think that is the end of the services." Charles gets up and turns off the telly.

"Scott, John, your mother has planned a surprise. She is going to perform some of the songs she used to sing here, at The Torch Café."

Charles stops for a moment and bends slightly over and exams John closely.

Then asks in a stern voice. "You do not have chewing gum in your mouth?"

"No Sir!" John quickly answered. "

"Good. Good."

Alice and Jenny laugh and Eric smiles. Charles goes over to where the record player is, picks up a record and starts to play it.

We hear the music for, "What do you do with a drunken sailor?

Jenny runs to the stage, not wanting to miss her music cue. She starts to sing, making funny faces to entertain her children. She shakes her head, with a comic look on her face.

"Oh, what do you do with a drunken sailor?"

The children laugh at her funny faces and clap. The stage lights start to dim, as we hear a few more lines of lyrics from Jenny and hear the children's laughter.

"What do you do with a drunken sailor, what do you do with a drunken sailor, early in the morning."

The End
David Jacquez